Between Whiles

Helen Jackson (H. H.)

1st WORLD
LIBRARY
Literary Society

Between Whiles

Helen Jackson (H. H.)

© 1st World Library – Literary Society, 2004
PO Box 2211
Fairfield, IA 52556
www.1stworldlibrary.org
First Edition

LCCN: 2004091197

Softcover ISBN: 1-59540-643-3
eBook ISBN: 1-59540-743-X

Purchase *"Between Whiles"*
as a traditional bound book at:
www.1stWorldLibrary.org/purchase.asp?ISBN=1-59540-643-3

1st World Library Literary Society is a nonprofit
organization dedicated to promoting literacy by:

- Creating a free internet library accessible from any
computer worldwide.
- Hosting writing competitions and offering book
publishing scholarships.

Readers interested in supporting literacy
through sponsorship, donations or
membership please contact:
literacy@1stworldlibrary.org
Check us out at: www.1stworldlibrary.org

CONTENTS

The Inn of the Golden Pear.

I.

Who buys? Who buys? 'Tis like a market-fair;
The hubbub rises deafening on the air:
The children spend their honest money there;
The knaves prowl out like foxes from a lair.

Who buys? Who sells? Alas, and still alas!
The children sell their diamond stones for glass;
The knaves their worthless stones for diamonds
pass.
He laughs who buys; he laughs who sells. Alas!

In the days when New England was only a group of
thinly settled wildernesses called "provinces," there
was something almost like the old feudal tenure of
lands there, and a relation between the rich land-owner
and his tenants which had many features in common
with those of the relation between margraves and
vassals in the days of Charlemagne.

Far up in the North, near the Canada line, there lived at
that time an eccentric old man, whose name is still to
be found here and there on the tattered parchments,
written "WILLAN BLAYCKE, Gentleman."

Tradition occupies itself a good deal with Willan Blaycke, and does not give his misdemeanors the go-by as it might have done if he had been either a poorer or a less clever man. Why he had crossed the seas and cast in his lot with the pious Puritans, nobody knew; it was certainly not because of sympathy with their God-reverencing faith and God-fearing lives, nor from any liking for hardships or simplicity of habits. He had gold enough, the stories say, to have bought all the land from the St. Johns to the Connecticut if he had pleased; and he had servants and horses and attire such as no governor in all the provinces could boast. He built himself a fine house out of stone, and the life he led in it was a scandal and a byword everywhere. For all that, there was not a man to be found who had not a good word to say for Willan Blaycke, and not a woman who did not look pleased and smile if he so much as spoke to her. He was generous, with a generosity so princely that there were many who said that he had no doubt come of some royal house. He gave away a farm to-day, and another to-morrow, and thought nothing of it; and when tenants came to him pleading that they were unable to pay their rent, he was never known to haggle or insist.

Naturally, with such ways as these he made havoc of his estates, vast as they were, and grew less and less rich year by year. However, there was enough of his land to last several generations out; and if he had married a decent woman for his wife, his posterity need never have complained of him. But this was what Willan Blaycke did, - and it is as much a mystery now as it doubtless was then, why he did it, - he married Jeanne Dubois, the daughter of a low-bred and evil-disposed Frenchman who kept a small inn on the Canadian frontier. Jeanne had a handsome but wicked face. She stood always at the bar, and served every man who came; and a great thing it was for the house, to be sure, that she had such bold black eyes, red cheeks, and a tongue even bolder than her glances. But there was not a farmer in all the north provinces who would have taken her to wife, not one, for she bore none too good a name; and men's speech about her, as soon as they had turned their backs and gone on their journeys, was quite opposite to the gallant and flattering things they said to her face in the bar. Some people said that Willan Blaycke was drunk when he married Jeanne, that she took him unawares by means of a base plot which her father and she had had in mind a long time. Others said that he was sober enough when he did it, only that he was like one out of his mind, - he sorrowed so for the loss of his only son, Willan, whom he had in the beginning of that year sent back to England to be taught in school.

He had brought the child out with him, - a little chap, with marvellously black eyes and yellow curls, who wore always the costliest of embroidered coats, which it was plain some woman's hand had embroidered for him; but whether the child's mother were dead or alive Willan Blaycke never told, and nobody dared ask.

That the boy needed a mother sadly enough was only too plain. Riding from county to county on his little white pony by his father's side, sitting up late at roystering feasts till he nodded in his chair, seeing all that rough men saw, and hearing all that rough men said, the child was in a fair way to be ruined outright; and so Willan Blaycke at last came to see, and one day, in a fit of unwonted conscientiousness and wisdom, he packed the poor sobbing little fellow off to England in charge of a trusty escort, and sternly made up his mind that the lad should not return till he was a man grown. It was only a few months after this that Jeanne Dubois became Mistress Willan Blaycke; so it seemed not improbable that the bereaved father's loneliness had had much to do with that extraordinary step.

Be that as it may, whether he were drunk or sober when he married her, he treated her as a gentleman should treat his wife, and did his best to make her a lady. She was always clad in a rich fashion; and a fine show she made in her scarlet petticoat and white hat with a streaming scarlet feather in it, riding high on her pillion behind Willan Blaycke on his great black horse, or sitting up straight and stiff in the swinging coach with gold on the panels, which he had bought for her in Boston at a sale of the effects of one of the disgraced and removed governors of the province of Massachusetts. If there had been any roads to speak of in those days, Jeanne Dubois would have driven from one end to the other of the land in her fine coach, so proud was she of its splendor; but even pride could not heal the bruises she got in jolting about in it, nor the terror she felt of being overturned. So she gradually left off using it, and consoled herself by keeping it standing in all good weather in full sight from the highway, that everybody might know she had it.

It was a sore trial to Jeanne that she had no children, - a sore trial also to her wicked old father, who had plotted that the great Blaycke estates should go down in the hands of his descendants. Not so Willan Blaycke. It was undoubtedly a consolation to him in his last days to think that his son Willan would succeed to everything, and the Dubois blood remain still in its own muddy channel. It is evident that before he died he had come to think coldly of his wife; for his

Helen Hunt Jackson

mention of her in his will was of the curtest, and his provision for her during her lifetime, though amply sufficient for her real needs, not at all in keeping with the style in which she had dwelt with him.

The exiled Willan had returned to America a year before his father's death. He was a quiet, well-educated, rather scholarly young man. It would be foolish to deny that his filial sentiment had grown cool during the long years of his absence, and that it received some violent shocks on his return to his father's house. But he was full of ambition, and soon saw the opening which lay before him for distinction and wealth as the ultimate owner of the Blaycke estates. To this end he bent all his energies. He had had in England a good legal education; he was a clear thinker and a ready speaker, and speedily made himself so well known and well thought of, that when his father died there were many who said it was well the old man had been taken away in time to leave the young Willan a property worthy of his talents and industry.

Willan had lived in his father's house more as a guest than as a son. To the woman who was his father's wife, and sat at the head of his father's table, he bore himself with a distant courtesy, which was far more irritating to her coarse nature than open antagonism would have been. But Jeanne Dubois was clever woman enough to comprehend her own inferiority to both father and son, and to avoid collisions with either. She had won what she had played for, and on the whole she had not been disappointed. As she had never loved her husband, she cared little that he did not love her; and as for the upstart of a boy with his fine airs, well, she would bide her time for that, Jeanne thought, - for it had never crossed Jeanne's mind that when her husband died she would not be still the mistress of the fine stone house and the gilt panelled coach, and have more money than she knew what to do with. Many malicious reveries she had indulged in as to how, when that time came, she would "send the fellow packing," "he shouldn't stay in her house a day." So, when it came to pass that the cards were turned, and it was Willan who said to her, on the morning after his father's funeral, "What are your plans, Madame?" Jeanne was for a few seconds literally dumb with anger and astonishment.

Then she poured out all the pent-up hatred of her vulgar soul. It was a horrible scene. Willan conducted himself throughout the interview with perfect calmness; the same impassable distance which had always been so exasperating to Jeanne was doubly so now. He treated her as if she were merely some dependant of the house, for whom he, as the executor of the will, was about to provide according to instructions.

"If I can't live in my own house," cried the angry woman, "I'll go back to my father and tend bar again; and how'll you like that?"

"It is purely immaterial to me, Madame," replied Willan, "where you live. I merely wish to know your address, that I may forward to you the quarterly payments of your annuity. I should think it probable," he added with an irony which was not thrown away on Jeanne, "that you would be happier among your own relations and in the occupations to which you were accustomed in your youth."

Jeanne was not deficient in spirit. As soon as she had

ascertained beyond a doubt that all that Willan had told her was true, and that there was no possibility of her ever getting from the estate anything except her annuity, she packed up all her possessions and left the house. No fine instinct had restrained her from laying, hands on everything to which she could be said to have a shadow of claim, - indeed, on many things to which she had not, - and even Willan himself, who had been prepared for her probable greed, was surprised when on returning to the house late one evening he found the piazza piled high from one end to the other with her boxes. Jeanne stood by with a defiant air, superintending the cording of the last one. She anticipated some remonstrance or inquiry from Willan, and was half disappointed when he passed by, giving no sign of having observed the boxes at all, and simply lifting his hat to her with his usual formality. The next morning, instead of the public vehicle which Jeanne had engaged to call for her, her own coach and the gray horses she had best liked were driven to the door. This unexpected tribute from Willan almost disarmed her for the moment. It was her coach almost more than her house which she had grieved to lose.

"Well, really, Mr. Willan," she exclaimed, "I never once thought of taking that, though there's no doubt about its being my own, and your father'd tell you so if he was here; and the horses too. He always said the grays were mine from the day he bought them. But I'm much obliged to you, I'm sure."

"You have no occasion to thank me, Madame," replied Willan, standing on the threshold of the house, pale with excitement at the prospect of immediate freedom from the presence of the coarse creature. "The coach is your own, and the horses; and if they had not been, I should not have permitted them to remain here."

"Oh ho!" sneered Jeanne, all her antagonism kindled afresh at this last gratuitous fling. "You needn't think you can get rid of everything that'll remind you of me, young man. You'll see me oftener than you like, at the Golden Pear. You'll have to stop there, as your father did before you." And Jeanne's black eyes snapped viciously as she drove off, her piles of boxes following slowly in two wagon-loads behind.

Willan was right in one thing. After the first mortification of returning to her father's house, a widow, disgraced by being pensioned off from her old home, had worn away, Jeanne was happier than she had ever been in her life. Her annuity, which was small for Mistress Willan Blaycke, was large for Jeanne, daughter of the landlord of the Golden Pear; and into that position she sank back at once, - so contentedly, too, that her father was continually reproaching her with a great lack of spirit. It was a sad come-down from his old air-castles for her and for himself, - he still the landlord of a shabby little inn, and Jeanne, stout and middle-aged, sitting again behind the bar as she had done fifteen years before. It was pretty hard. So long as he knew that Jeanne was living in her fine house as Mistress Blaycke he had been content, in spite of Willan Blaycke's having sternly forbidden him ever to show his face there. But this last downfall was too much. Victor Dubois ground his teeth and swore many oaths over it. But no swearing could alter things; and after a while Victor himself began to take comfort in having Jeanne back again. "And not a bit spoiled," as he would say to his cronies, "by all the fine ways, to which she had never taken; thanks to God, Jeanne was as good a girl yet as ever." - "And as handsome too," the politic cronies would add.

The Golden Pear was a much more attractive place since Jeanne had come back. She was a good housekeeper, and she had learned much in Willan Blaycke's house. Moreover, she was a generous creature, and did not in the least mind spending a few dollars here and there to make things tidier and more comfortable.

A few weeks after Jeanne's return to the inn there appeared in the family a new and by no means insignificant member. This was the young Victorine Dubois, who was a daughter, they said, of Victor Dubois's son Jean, the twin brother of Jeanne. He had gone to Montreal many years ago, and had been moderately prosperous there as a wine-seller in a small way. He had been dead now for two years, and his widow, being about to marry again, was anxious to get the young Victorine off her hands. So the story ran, and on the surface it looked probable enough. But Montreal was not a great way off from the parish of St. Urbans, in which stood Victor Dubois's inn; there were men coming and going often who knew the city, and who looked puzzled when it was said in their hearing that Victorine was the eldest child of Jean Dubois the wine-seller. She had been kept at a convent all these years, old Victor said, her father being determined that at least one of his children should be well educated.

Nobody could gainsay this, and Mademoiselle Victorine certainly had the air of having been much better trained and taught than most girls in her station. But somehow, nobody quite knew why, the tale of her being Jean Dubois's daughter was not believed. Suspicions and at last rumors were afloat that she was an illegitimate child of Jeanne's, born a few years before her marriage to Willan Blaycke.

Nothing easier, everybody knew, than for Mistress Willan Blaycke to have supported half a dozen illegitimate children, if she had had them, on the money her husband gave her so lavishly; and there was old Victor, as ready and unscrupulous a go-between as ever an unscrupulous woman needed. These rumors gained all the easier credence because Victorine bore so striking a resemblance to her "Aunt Jeanne." On the other hand, this ought not to have been taken as proof any more one way than the other; for there were plenty of people who recollected very well that in the days when little Jean and Jeanne toddled about together as children, nobody but their mother could tell them apart, except by their clothes. So the winds of gossiping breaths blew both ways at once in the matter, and it was much discussed for a time. But like all scandals, as soon as it became an old story nobody cared whether it were false or true; and before Victorine had been a year at the Golden Pear, the question of her relationship there was rarely raised.

One thing was certain, that no mother could have been fonder or more devoted to a child than Jeanne was to her niece; and everybody said so, - some more civilly, some maliciously. Her pride in the girl's beauty was touching to see. She seemed to have forgotten that she was ever a beauty herself; and she had no need to do this, for Jeanne was not yet forty, and many men found her piquant and pleasing still. But all her vanity seemed now to be transferred to Victorine. It was Victorine who was to have all the fine gowns and ornaments; Victorine who must go to the dances and fêtes in costumes which were the wonder and the envy

Helen Hunt Jackson

of all the girls in the region; Victorine who was to have everything made easy and comfortable for her in the house; and above all, - and here the mother betrayed herself, for mother she was; the truth may as well be told early as late in our story, - most of all, it was Victorine who was to be kept away from the bar, and to be spared all contact with the rough roysterers who frequented the Golden Pear.

Very ingenious were Jeanne's excuses for these restrictions on her niece's liberty. Still more ingenious her explanations of the occasional exceptions she made now and then in favor of some well-to-do young farmer of the neighborhood, or some traveller in whom her alert maternal eye detected a possible suitor for Victorine's hand. Victorine herself was not so fastidious. She was young, handsome, overflowing with vitality, and with no more conscience or delicacy than her mother had had before her. If the whole truth had been known concerning the last four years of her life in the convent, it would have considerably astonished those good Catholics, if any such there be, who still believe that convents are sacred retreats filled with the chaste and the devout. Victorine Dubois at the age of eighteen, when her grandfather took her home to his house, was as well versed a young woman in the ways and the wiles of love-making as if she had been free to come and go all her life. And that this knowledge had been gained surreptitiously, in stolen moments and brief experiences at the expense of the whole of her reverence for religion, the whole of her faith in men's purity, was not poor Victorine's fault, only her misfortune; but the result was no less disastrous to her morals. She went out of the convent as complete a little hypocrite as ever told beads and repeated prayers. Only a certain sort of infantile superstitiousness of nature remained in her, and made her cling to the forms, in which, though she knew they did not mean what they pretended, she suspected there might be some sort of mechanical efficacy at last; like the partly undeceived disciple and assistant of a master juggler, who is not quite sure that there may not be a supernatural power behind some of the tricks. Beyond an overflowing animal vitality, and a passion for having men make love to her, there really was not much of Victorine. But it is wonderful how far these two qualities can pass in a handsome woman for other and nobler ones. The animal life so keen, intense, sensuous, can seem like cleverness, wit, taste; the passion for receiving homage from men can make a woman graceful, amiable, and alluring. Some of the greatest passions the world has ever seen have been inspired in men by just such women as this.

Victorine was not without accomplishments and some smattering of knowledge. She had read a good deal of French, and chattered it like the true granddaughter of a Normandy *propriétaire*. She sang, in a half-rude, half-melodious way, snatches of songs which sounded better than they really were, she sang them with so much heartiness and abandon. She embroidered exquisitely, and had learned the trick of making many of the pretty and useless things at which nuns work so patiently to fill up their long hours. She had an insatiable love of dress, and attired herself daily in successions of varied colors and shapes merely to look at herself in the glass, and on the chance of showing herself to any stray traveller who might come.

The inn had been built in a piecemeal fashion by Victor Dubois himself, and he had been unconsciously guided all the while by his memories of the old farmhouse in Normandy in which he was born; so that the house really looked more like Normandy than like America. It had on one corner a square tower, which began by being a shed attached to the kitchen, then was promoted to bearing up a chamber for grain, and at last was topped off by a fine airy room, projecting on all sides over the other two, and having great casement windows reaching close up to the broad, hanging eaves. A winding staircase outside led to what had been the grain-chamber: this was now Jeanne's room. The room above was Victorine's, and she reached it only by a narrow, ladder-like stairway from her mother's bedroom; so the young lady's movements were kept well in sight, her mother thought. It was an odd thing that it never occurred to Jeanne how near the sill of Victorine's south window was to the stout railing of the last broad platform of the outside staircase. This railing had been built up high, and was partly roofed over, making a pretty place for pots of flowers in summer; and Victorine never looked so well anywhere as she did leaning out of her window and watering the flowers which stood there. Many a flirtation went on between this casement window and the courtyard below, where all the travellers were in the habit of standing and talking with the ostlers, and with old Victor himself, who was not the landlord to leave his ostlers to do as they liked with horses and grain, - many a flirtation, but none that meant or did any harm; for with all her wildness and love of frolic, Mademoiselle Victorine never lost her head. Deep down in her heart she had an ambition which she never confessed even to her aunt Jeanne. She had read enough romances to believe that it was by no means an impossible thing that a landlord's daughter should marry a gentleman; and to marry a gentleman, if she married at all, Victorine was fully resolved. She never tired of questioning her aunt about the details of her life in Willan Blaycke's house; and she sometimes gazed for hours at the gilt-panelled coach, which on all fine days stood in the courtyard of the Golden Pear, the wonder of all rustics. On the rare occasions when her aunt went abroad in this fine vehicle, Victorine sat by her side in an ecstasy of pride and delight. It seemed to her that to be the owner of such a coach as that, to live in a fine house, and have a fine gentleman for one's husband must be the very climax of bliss. She wondered much at her aunt's contentment in her present estate.

"How canst thou bear it, Aunt Jeanne?" she said sometimes. "How canst thou bear to live as we live here, - to be in the bar-room with the men, and to sit always in the smoke, after the fine rooms and the company thou hadst for so long?"

"Bah!" Jeanne would reply. "It's little thou knowest of that fine company. I had like to die of weariness more often than I was gay in it; and as for fine rooms, I care nothing for them."

"But thy husband, Aunt Jeanne," Victorine once ventured to say, - "surely thou wert not weary when he was with thee?"

Jeanne's face darkened. "Keep a civiller tongue in thy head," she replied, "than to be talking to widows of the husbands they have buried. He was a good man, Willan Blaycke, - a good man; but I liked him not overmuch, though we lived not in quarrelling. He went his ways, as men go, and I let him be."

Victorine's curiosity was by no means satisfied. She

Helen Hunt Jackson

asked endless questions of all whom she met who could tell her anything about her aunt's husband. Very much she regretted that she had not been taken from the convent before this strange, free-hearted, rollicking gentleman had died. She would have managed affairs better, she thought, than Aunt Jeanne had done. Romantic visions of herself as his favorite flitted through her brain.

"Why didst thou not send for me sooner to come to thee, Aunt Jeanne," she said, "that I too might have seen the life in the great stone house?"

A sudden flush covered Jeanne's face. Was she never to hear the end of troublesome questions about the past?

"Wilt thou never have done with it?" she said, half angrily. "Has it never been said in thy hearing how that my husband would not permit even my father to come inside of his house, much less one no nearer than thou?" And Jeanne eyed Victorine sharply, with a suspicion which was wholly uncalled for. Nobody had ever been bold or cruel enough to suggest to Victorine any doubts regarding her birth. The girl was indignant. She had never known before that her grandfather had been thus insulted.

"What had grandfather done?" she cried. "Was he not thy husband's father, too, being thine? How dared thy husband treat him so?"

Jeanne was silent for a few moments. A latent sense of justice to her dead husband restrained her from assenting to Victorine's words. "Nay," she said; "there are many things thou canst not understand. Thy grandfather never complained. Willan Blaycke treated me most fairly while he lived; and if it had not been for the boy, I would have had thee in the stone house to-day, and had all my rights."

"Why did the boy hate thee?" asked Victorine. "What is he like?"

"As like to a magpie as one magpie is to another," said Jeanne, bitterly; "with his fine French cloth of black, and his white ruffles, and his long words in his mouth. Ah, but him I hate! It is to him we owe it all."

"Dwells he now in the great house alone?" said Victorine.

"Ay, that he does, - alone with his books, of which he has about as many as there are leaves on the trees; one could not so much as step or sit for a book in one's way. I did hear that he has now with him another of his own order, and that the two are riding all over the country, marking out the lines anew of all the farms, and writing new bonds which are so much harder on men than the old ones were. Bah! but he has the soul of a miser in him, for all his handsome face!"

"Is he then so very handsome, Aunt Jeanne?" said Victorine, eagerly.

"Ay, ay, child. I'll give him his due for that, evilly as he has treated me. He is a handsomer man than his father was; and when his father and I were married there was not a woman in the provinces that did not say I had carried off the handsomest man that ever strode a horse. I'd like to have had thee see me, too, in that day, child. I was counted as handsome as he, though thou'dst never think it now."

"But I would think it!" cried Victorine, hotly and loyally. "What ails thee, Aunt Jeanne? Did I not hear Father Hennepin himself saying to thee only yesterday that thou wert comelier to-day than ever? and he saw thee married, he told me."

"Tut, tut, child!" replied Jeanne, looking pleased. "None know better than the priests how to speak idle words to women. But what was he telling thee? How came it that he spoke of the time when I was married?" added Jeanne, again suspicious.

"It was I that asked him," replied Victorine. "I wish always so much that I had been with thee instead of in the convent, dear aunt. Does this son of thy husband, this handsome young man who is so like unto a magpie, - does he never in his journeyings come this way?"

"Ay, often," replied Jeanne. "I know that he must, because a large part of his estate lies beyond the border and joins on to this parish. It was that which brought his father here, in the beginning, and there is no other inn save this for miles up and down the border where he can tarry; but it is likely that he will sooner lie out in the fields than sleep under this roof, because I am here. I had looked to say my mind to him as often as he came; and that it would be a sore thing to him to see his father's wife in the bar, I know beyond a doubt. I have often said to myself what a comfortable spleen I should experience when I might courtesy to him and say, 'What would you be pleased to take, sir?' But I think he is minded to rob me of that pleasure, for it is certain he must have ridden this way before now."

"I have a mind to burn a candle to the Virgin," said Victorine, slowly, "that he may come here. I would like for once to set my eyes on his face."

An unwonted earnestness in Victorine's tone and a still more unwonted seriousness in her face arrested Jeanne's attention.

"What is it to thee to see him or not to see him, eh? What is it thou hast in thy silly head. If thou thinkest thou couldst win him over to take us back to live in his house again, - which is my own house, to be sure, if I had my rights, - thy wits are wool-gathering, I can tell thee that," cried Jeanne. "He has the pride of ten thousand devils in him. There was that in his face when I drove away from the door, - and he standing with his head uncovered too, - which I tell thee if I had been a man I could have killed him for. He take us back! He! he!" And Jeanne laughed a bitter laugh at the bare idea of the thing.

"I had not thought of any such thing, Aunt Jeanne," replied Victorine, still speaking slowly, and still with a dreamy expression on her face, as she leaned out of the window and began idly plucking the blossoms from a bough of the big pear-tree, which was now all white with flowers and buzzing with bees. "Dost thou not think the bees steal a little sweet that ought to go into the fruit?" continued the artful girl, who did not choose that her aunt should question her any further as to the reason of her desire to see Willan Blaycke. "I remember that once Father Anselmo at the convent said to me he thought so. There was a vine of the wild grape which ran all over the wall between the cloister and the convent; and when it was in bloom the air sickened one, and thou couldst hardly go near the wall

Helen Hunt Jackson

for the swarming bees that were drinking the honey from the flowers. And Father Anselmo said one evening that they were thieves; they stole sweet which ought to go into the grapes."

This was a clever diversion. It turned Jeanne's thoughts at once away from Willan Blaycke, but it did not save Mademoiselle Victorine from a catechising quite as sharp as she was in danger of on the other subject.

"And what wert thou doing talking with a priest in the garden at night?" cried Jeanne, fiercely. "Is that the way maidens are trained in a convent! Shame on thee, Victorine! what hast thou revealed?"

"The Virgin forbid," answered Victorine, piously, racking her brains meanwhile for a ready escape from this dilemma, and trying in her fright to recall precisely what she had just said. "I said not that he told it to me in the garden; it was in the confessional that he said it. I had confessed to him the grievous sin of a horrible rage I had been in when one of the bees had stung me on the lip as I was gathering the cool vine leaves to lay on the good Sister Clarice's forehead, who was ill with a fever."

"Eh, eh!" said Jeanne, relieved; "was that it? I thought it could not be thou wert in the garden in the evening hours, and with a priest."

"Oh no," said Victorine, demurely. "It was not permitted to converse with the priests except in the chapel." And choking back an amused little laugh she bounded to the ladder-like stairway and climbed up into her own room.

"Saints! what an ankle the girl has, to be sure!" thought Jeanne, as she watched Victorine's shapely legs slowly vanishing up the stair. "What has filled her head so full of that upstart Willan, I wonder!"

A thought struck Jeanne; the only wonder was it had never struck her before. In her sudden excitement she sprung from her chair, and began to walk rapidly up and down the floor. She pressed her hand to her forehead; she tore open the handkerchief which was crossed on her bosom; her eyes flashed; her cheeks grew red; she breathed quicker.

"The girl's handsome enough to turn any man's head, and twice as clever as I ever was," she thought.

She sat down in her chair again. The idea which had occurred to her was over-whelming. She spoke aloud and was unconscious of it.

"Ah, but that would be a triumph!" she said. "Who knows? who knows?"

"Victorine!" she called; "Victorine!"

"Yes, aunt," replied Victorine.

"There's plenty of honey left in the flowers to keep pears sweet after the bees are dead," said Jeanne, mischievously, and went downstairs chuckling over her new secret thought. "I'll never let the child know I've thought of such a thing," she mused, as she took her accustomed seat in the bar. "I'll bide my time. Strange things have happened, and may happen again."

"What a queer speech of Aunt Jeanne's!" thought

Victorine at her casement window. "What a fool I was to have said anything about Father Anselmo! Poor fellow! I wonder why he doesn't run away from the monastery!"

II.

The south wind's secret, when it blows,
Oh, what man knows?
How did it turn the rose's bud
Into a rose?
What went before, no garden shows;
Only the rose!

What hour the bitter north wind blows,
The south wind knows.
Why did it turn the rose's bud
Into a rose?
Alas, to-day the garden shows
A dying rose!

Jeanne had not to wait long. It was only a few days after this conversation with Victorine, - the big pear-tree was still snowy-white with bloom, and the tireless bees still buzzed thick among its boughs, - when Jeanne, standing in the doorway at sunset, saw two riders approaching the inn. At her first glance she recognized Willan Blaycke. Jeanne's mind moved quickly. In the twinkling of an eye she had sprung back into the bar-room, and said to her father, -

"Father, father, be quick! Here comes Willan Blaycke riding; and another, an old man, with him. Thou must tend the bar; for hand so much as a glass of gin to that man will I never. I shut myself up till he is gone."

"Nay, nay, Jeanne," replied Victor; "I'll turn him from my door. He's to get no lodging under this roof, he nor his, - I promise you that." And Victor was bustling angrily to the door.

This did not suit Mistress Jeanne at all. In great dismay inwardly, but outwardly with slow and smooth-spoken accents, as if reflecting discreetly, she replied, "He might do me great mischief if he were angered, father. All the moneys go through his hand. I think it is safer to speak him fair. He hath the devil's own temper if he be opposed in the smallest thing. It has cost him sore enough, I'll be bound, to find himself here at sundown, and beholden to thee for shelter; it is none of his will to come, I know that well enough. Speak him fair, father, speak him fair; it is a silly fowl that pecks at the hand which holds corn. I will hide myself till he is away, though, for I misgive me that I should be like to fly out at him."

"But, Jeanne - " persisted Victor. But Jeanne was gone.

"Speak him fair, father; take no note that aught is amiss," she called back from the upper stair, from which she was vanishing into her chamber. "I will send Victorine to wait at the supper. He hath never seen her, and need not to know that she is of our kin at all,"

"Humph!" muttered Victor. "Small doubt to whom the girl is kin, if a man have eyes in his head." And he would have argued the point longer with Jeanne, but he had no time left, for the riders had already turned into the courtyard, and were giving their horses in charge to the white-headed ostler Benoit. Benoit had served in the Golden Pear for a quarter of a century. He had served Victor Dubois's father in Normandy, had come with his young master to America, and was nominally his servant still. But if things had gone by their right names at the Golden Pear, old Benoit would not have been called servant for many a year back. Not a secret in that household which Benoit had not shared; not a plot he had not helped on. At Jeanne's marriage he was the only witness except Father Hennepin; and there were some who recollected still with what extraordinary chuckles of laughter Benoit had walked away from the chapel after that ceremony had been completed. To the young Victorine Benoit had been devoted ever since her coming to the inn. Whenever she appeared in sight the old man came to gaze on her, and stood lingering and admiring as long as she remained.

"Thou art far handsomer than thy mother ever was," he had said to her one morning soon after her arrival.

"Oh, didst thou know my mother, then, when she was young?" cried Victorine. "She is not handsome now, though she is newly wed; when she came to see me in the convent, I thought her very ugly. When didst thou know her, Benoit?"

Benoit was very red in the face, and began to toss straw vigorously as he looked away from Victorine and answered: "It was but once that I had sight of her, when Master Jean brought her here after they were married. Thou dost not favor her in the least. Thou art like Master Jean."

"And the saints know that that last is the holy truth, whatever the rest may be," thought Benoit, as he bustled about the courtyard.

"But thy tongue is the tongue of an imbecile," said Victor, following him into the stable.

"Ay, that it is, sir," replied Benoit, humbly. "I had like to have bitten it off before I had finished speaking; but no harm came."

"Not this time," replied Victor; "but the next thou might not be so well let off. The girl has a sharper wit than she shows ordinarily. She hath learned too well the ways of convents. I trust her not wholly, Benoit. Keep thy eyes open, Benoit. We'll not have her go the ways of her mother if it can be helped." And the worldly and immoral old grandfather turned on his heel with a wicked laugh.

Benoit had never seen young Willan Blaycke, but he knew him at his first glance.

"The son!" he muttered under his breath, as he saw him alight. "Is he to be lodged here? I doubt." And Benoit looked about for Victor, who was nowhere to be seen. Slowly and with a surly face he came forward to take the horses.

"What're you about, old man? Wear you shoes of lead? Take our horses, and see you to it they are well rubbed down before they have aught to eat or drink. We have ridden more than ten leagues since the noon," cried the elder of the two travellers.

"And ought to have ridden more," said the younger in an undertone. It was, as Jeanne had said, a sore thing to Willan Blaycke to be forced to seek a night's shelter in the Golden Pear.

"Tut, tut!" said the other, "what odds! It is a whimsey, a weakness of yours, boy. What's the woman to you?"

Victor Dubois, who had come up now, heard these words, and his swarthy cheek was a shade darker. Benoit, who had lingered till he should receive a second order from the master of the inn as to the strangers' horses, exchanged a quick glance with Victor, while he said in a respectful tone, "Two horses, sir, for the night." The glance said, "I know who the man is; shall we keep him?"

"Ay, Benoit," Victor answered; "see that Jean gives them a good rubbing at once. They have been hard ridden, poor beasts!" While Victor was speaking these words his eyes said to Benoit, "Bah! It is even so; but we dare not do otherwise than treat him fair."

"Will you be pleased to walk in, gentlemen; and what shall I have the honor of serving for your supper?" he continued. "We have some young pigeons, if your worships would like them, fat as partridges, and still a bottle or two left of our last autumn's cider."

"By all means, landlord, by all means, let us have them, roasted on a spit, man, - do you hear? - roasted on a spit, and let your cook lard them well with fat bacon; there is no bird so fat but a larding doth help it for my eating," said the elder man, rubbing his hands and laughing more and more cheerily as his companion looked each moment more and more glum.

"No, I'll not go in," said Willan, as Victor threw open the door into the bar-room. "It suits me better to sit here under the trees until supper is ready." And he threw himself down at the foot of the great pear-tree. He feared to see Jeanne sitting in the bar, as she had threatened. The ground was showered thick with the soft white petals of the blossoms, which were now past their prime. Willan picked up a handful of them and tossed them idly in the air. As he did so, a shower of others came down on his face, thick, fast; they half blinded him for a moment. He sprung to his feet and looked up. It was like looking into a snowy cloud. He saw nothing. "Some bird flying through," he thought, and lay down again.

"Ah! luck for the bees,
The flowers are in flower;
Luck for the bees in spring.
Ah me, but the flowers, they die in an hour;
No summer is fair as the spring.
Ah! luck for the bees;
The honey in flowers
Is highest when they are on wing!"

came in a gay Provençal melody from the pear-tree above Willan's head, and another shower of white petals fell on his face.

"Good God!" said Willan Blaycke, under his breath, "what witchcraft is going on here? what girl's voice is that?" And he sprang again to his feet.

The voice died slowly away; the singer was moving farther off, -

"Ah! woe for the bees,
The flowers are dead;
No summer is fair as the spring.
Ah me, but the honey is thick in the comb;
'Tis a long time now since spring.
Ah, woe for the bees
That honey is sweet,
Is sweeter than anything!"

"Sweeter than anything, - sweeter than anything!" the voice, grown faint now, repeated this refrain over and over, as the syllables of sound died away.

It was Victorine going very slowly down the staircase from her room into Jeanne's. And it was Victorine who had accidentally brushed the pear-tree boughs as she watered her plants on the roof of the outside stairway. She did not see Willan lying on the ground underneath, and she did not think that Willan might be hearing her song; and yet was her head full of Willan Blaycke as she went down the staircase, and not a little did she quake at the thought of seeing him below.

Jeanne had come breathless to her room, crying, "Victorine! Victorine! That son of my husband's of whom we were talking, young Willan Blaycke, is at the door, - he, and an old man with him; and they must perforce stay here all night. Now, it would be a shame I could in no wise bear to stand and serve him at supper. Wilt thou not do it in my stead? there are but the two." And the wily Jeanne pretended to be greatly distressed, as she sank into a chair and went on: "In truth, I do not believe I can look on his face at all. I will keep my room till he have gone his way, - the villain, the upstart, that I may thank for all my trouble! Oh, it brings it all back again, to see his face!" And Jeanne actually brought a tear or two into her wily eyes.

The no less wily Victorine tossed her head and replied: "Indeed, then, and the waiting on him is no more to my liking than to thine own, Aunt Jeanne! I did greatly desire to see his face, to see what manner of man he could be that would turn his father's widow out of her house; but I think Benoit may hand the gentleman his wine, not I." And Victorine sauntered saucily to the window and looked out.

"A plague on all their tempers!" thought Jeanne, impatiently. Her plans seemed to be thwarted when she least expected it. For a few moments she was silent, revolving in her mind the wisdom of taking Victorine into her counsels, and confiding to her the motive she had for wishing her to be seen by Willan Blaycke. But she dreaded lest this might defeat her object by making the girl self-conscious. Jeanne was perplexed; and in her perplexity her face took on an expression as if she were grieved. Victorine, who was much dismayed by her aunt's seeming acquiescence in her refusal to serve the supper, exclaimed now, -

"Nay, nay, Aunt Jeanne, do not look grieved. I will indeed go down and serve the supper, if thou takest it so to heart. The man is nothing to me, that I need fear to see him."

"Thou art a good girl," replied Jeanne, much relieved, and little dreaming how she had been gulled by Mademoiselle Victorine, - "thou art a good girl, and thou shalt have my lavender-colored paduasoy gown if thou wilt lay thyself out to see that all is at its best, both in the bedrooms and for the supper. I would have Willan Blaycke perceive that one may live as well outside of his house as in it. And, Victorine," she added, with an attempt at indifference in her tone, "wear thy white gown thou hadst on last Sunday. It pleased me better than any gown thou hast worn this year, - that, and thy black silk apron with the red lace; they become thee."

So Victorine had arrayed herself in the white gown; it

was of linen quaintly woven, with a tiny star thrown up in the pattern, and shone like damask. The apron was of heavy black silk, trimmed all around with crimson lace, and crimson lace on the pockets. A crimson rose in Victorine's black hair and crimson ribbons at her throat and on her sleeves completed the toilet. It was ravishing; and nobody knew it better than Mademoiselle Victorine herself, who had toiled many an hour in the convent making the crimson lace for the precise purpose of trimming a black apron with it, if ever she escaped from the convent, and who had chosen out of fifty rose-bushes at the last Parish Fair the one whose blossoms matched her crimson lace. There is a picture still to be seen of Victorine in this costume; and many a handsome young girl, having copied the costume exactly for a fancy ball, has looked from the picture to herself and from herself to the picture, and gone to the ball dissatisfied, thinking in her heart, -

"After all, I don't look half as well in it as that French girl did."

As Victorine came leisurely down the stairs, half singing, half chanting, her little song, Jeanne looked at her in admiration.

"Well, and if either of the men have an eye for a pretty girl clad in attire that becomes her, they can look at thee, my Victorine. That black apron will go well with the lavender paduasoy also."

"That it will, Aunt Jeanne," answered Victorine, her face glowing with pleasure. "I can never thank thee enough. I did not think ever to have the paduasoy for my own."

"All my gowns are for thee," said Jeanne, in a voice of great tenderness. "I shall presently take to the wearing of black; it better suits my years. Thou canst be young; it is enough. I am an old woman."

Victorine bent over and kissed her aunt, and whispered: "Fie on thee, Aunt Jeanne! The Father Hennepin does not think thee an old woman; neither Pierre Gaspard from the mill. I hear the men when they are talking under my window of thee. Thou knowest thou mightest wed any day if thou hadst the mind."

Jeanne shook her head. "That I have not, then," she said. "I keep the name of Willan Blaycke for all that of any man hereabouts which can be offered to me. Thou art the one to wed, not I. But far off be that day," she added hastily; "thou art young for it yet."

"Ay," replied the artful young maiden, "that am I, and I think I will be old before any man make a drudge of me. I like my freedom better. And now will I go down and serve thy stepson, - the handsome magpie, the reader of books." And with a mocking laugh Victorine bounded down the staircase and went into the kitchen. Her grandfather was running about there in great confusion, from dresser to fireplace, to table, to pantry, back and forth, breathless and red in the face. The pigeons were sputtering before the fire, and the odor of the frying bacon filled the place.

"Diable! Girl, out of this!" he cried; "this is no place for thee. Go to thine aunt."

"She did bid me come and serve the supper for the strangers," replied Victorine. "She herself will not come down."

"Go to the devil! Thou shalt not, and it is I that say it," shouted Victor; and Victorine, terrified, fled back to Jeanne, and reported her grandfather's words.

Poor Jeanne was at her wit's end now. "Why said he that?" she asked.

"I know not," replied Victorine, demurely. "He was in one of his great rages, and I do think that the pigeons are fast burning, by the smell."

"Bah!" cried Jeanne, in disgust. "Is this a house to live in, where one cannot be let down from one's chamber except in sight of the highway? Run, Victorine! Look over and see if the strangers be in sight. I must go down to the kitchen. I would a witch were at hand with a broom or a tail of a mare. I'd mount and down the chimney, I warrant me!"

Laughing heartily, Victorine ran to reconnoitre. "There is none in sight," she cried. "Thou canst come down. A man is asleep under the pear-tree, but I think not he is one of them."

Jeanne ran quickly down the stairs, followed by Victorine, who, as she entered the kitchen again, took up her position in one corner, and stood leaning against the wall, tapping her pretty little black slippers with their crimson bows impatiently on the floor. Jeanne drew her father to one side, and whispered in his ear. He retorted angrily, in a louder tone. Not a look or tone was lost on Victorine. Presently the old man, shrugging his shoulders, went back to the pigeons, and began to turn the spit, muttering to himself in French. Jeanne had conquered.

"Thy grandfather is in a rage," she said to Victorine, "because we must give meat and drink to the man who has treated me so ill; that is why he did not wish thee to serve. But I have persuaded him that it is needful that we do all we can to keep Willan Blaycke well disposed to us. He might withhold from me all my money if he so chose; and he is rich, and we are but poor people. We could not find any redress. So do thou take care and treat him as if thou hadst never heard aught against him from me. It will lie with thee, child, to see that he goes not away angered; for thy grandfather is in a mood when the saints themselves could not hold his tongue if he have a mind to speak. Keep thou out of his sight till supper be ready. I stay here till all is done."

Between the kitchen and the common living-room, which was also the dining-room, was a long dark passage-way, at one end of which was a small storeroom. Here Victorine took refuge, to wait till her aunt should call her to serve the supper. The window of this storeroom was wide open. The shutter had fallen off the hinges several days before, and Benoit had forgotten to put it up. Victorine seated herself on a cider cask close to the window, and leaning her head against the wall began to sing again in a low tone. She had a habit of singing at all times, and often hardly knew that she sang at all. The Provençal melody was still running in her head.

> "Ah! luck for the bees,
> The flowers are in flower;
> Luck for the bees in spring.
> Ah me, but the flowers, they die in an hour;
> No summer is fair as the spring.
> Ah! luck for the bees;

The honey in flowers
Is highest when they are on wing!"

she sang. Then suddenly breaking off she began
singing a wild, sad melody of another song: -

"The sad spring rain,
It has come at last.
The graves lie plain,
And the brooks run fast;
And drip, drip, drip,
Falls the sad spring rain;
And tears fall fresh,
In the sad spring air,
From lovers' eyes,
On the graves laid bare."

It was very dark in the storeroom; it was dark out of
doors. The moon had been up for an hour, but the sky
was overcast thick with clouds. Willan Blaycke was
still asleep under the pear-tree. His head was only a
few feet from the storeroom window. The sound of
Victorine's singing reached his ears, but did not at first
waken him, only blended confusedly with his dreams.
In a few seconds, however, he waked, sprang to his
feet, and looked about him in bewilderment. Out of the
darkness, seemingly within arm's reach, came the low
sweet notes, -

"And drip, drip, drip,
Falls the sad spring rain;
And tears fall fresh,
In the sad spring air,
From lovers' eyes,
On the graves laid bare."

Groping his way in the direction from which the voice came, Willan stumbled against the wall of the house, and put his hand on the window-sill. "Who sings in here?" he cried, fumbling in the empty space.

"Holy Mother!" shrieked Victorine, and ran out of the storeroom, letting the door shut behind her with all its force. The noise echoed through the inn, and waked Willan's friend, who was also taking a nap in one of the old leather-cushioned high-backed chairs in the bar-room. Rubbing his eyes, he came out to look for Willan. He met him on the threshold.

"Ah!" he said, "where have you been all this time? I have slept in a chair, and am vastly rested."

"The Lord only knows where I have been," answered Willan, laughing. "I too have slept; but a woman with a voice like the voice of a wild bird has been singing strange melodies in my ear."

The elder man smiled. "The dreams of young men," he said, "are wont to have the sound of women's voices in them."

"This was no dream," retorted Willan. "She was so near me I heard the panting breath with which she cried out and fled when I made a step towards her."

"Gentlemen, will it please you to walk in to supper?" said Victor, appearing in the doorway with a clean white apron on, and no trace, in his smiling and obsequious countenance, of the rage in which he had been a few minutes before.

A second talk with Jeanne after Victorine had left the

kitchen had produced a deep impression on Victor's mind. He was now as eager as Jeanne herself for the meeting between Victorine and Willan Blaycke.

The pigeons were not burned, after all. Most savory did they smell, and Willan Blaycke and his friend fell to with a will.

"Saidst thou not thou hadst some of thy famous pear cider left, landlord?" asked Willan.

"Ay, sir, my granddaughter has gone to draw it; she will be here in a trice."

As he spoke the door opened, and Victorine entered, bearing in her left hand a tray with two curious old blue tankards on it; in her right hand a gray stone jug with blue bands at its neck. Both the jug and the tankards had come over from Normandy years ago. Victorine raised her eyes, and looking first at Willan, then at his friend, went immediately to the older man, and courtesying gracefully, set her tray down on the table by his side, and filled the two tankards. The cider was like champagne; it foamed and sparkled. The old man eyed it keenly.

"This looks like the cidre mousseux I drank at Littry," he said, and taking up his tankard tossed it off at a draught. "Tastes like it, too, by Jove!" he said. "Old man, out of what fruits in this bleak country dost thou conjure such a drink?"

Victor smiled. Praise of the cider of the Golden Pear went to his heart of hearts. "Monsieur has been in Calvados," he said. "It is kind of him then to praise this poor drink of mine, which would be but scorned there.

There is not a warm enough sunshine to ripen our pears here to their best, and the variety is not the same; but such as they are, I have an orchard of twenty trees, and it is by reason of them that the inn has its name."

Willan was not listening to this conversation. He held his fork, with a bit of untasted pigeon on it, uplifted in one hand; with the other he drummed nervously on the table. His eyes were riveted on Victorine, who stood behind the old man's chair, her soft black eyes glancing quietly from one thing to another on the table to see if all were right. Willan's gaze did not escape the keen eyes of Victorine's grandfather. Chuckling inwardly, he assumed an expression of great anxiety, and coming closer to Willan's chair said in a deprecating tone, -

"Are not the pigeons done to your liking, sir? You do not eat."

Willan started, dropped his fork, then hastily took it up again.

"Yes, yes," he said, "that they are; done to a turn." And he fell to eating again. But do what he would, he could not keep his eyes off the face of the girl. If she moved, his gaze followed her about the room, as straight as a steel follows on after a magnet; and when she stood still, he cast furtive glances that way each minute. In very truth, he might well be forgiven for so doing. Not often does it fall to the lot of men to see a more bewitching face than the face of Victorine Dubois. Many a woman might be found fairer and of a nobler cast of feature; but in the countenance of Victorine Dubois was an unaccountable charm wellnigh independent of feature, of complexion, of all which goes to the ordinary summing up of a woman's beauty.

There was in the glance of her eye a something, I know not what, which no man living could wholly resist. It was at once defiant and alluring, tender and mocking, artless and mischievous. No man could make it out; no man might see it twice alike in the space of an hour. No more was the girl herself twice alike in an hour, or a day, for that matter. She was far more like some frolicsome creature of the woods than like a mortal woman. The quality of wildness which Willan had felt in her voice was in her nature. Neither her grandfather nor her mother had in the least comprehended her during the few months she had lived with them. A certain gentleness of nature, which was far more physical than mental, far more an idle nonchalance than recognition of relations to others, had blinded them to her real capriciousness and selfishness. They rarely interfered with her, or observed her with any discrimination. Their love was content with her surface of good humor, gayety, and beauty; she was an ever-present delight and pride to them both, and that she might only partially reciprocate this fondness never crossed their minds. They did not realize that during all these eighteen years that they had been caring, planning, and plotting for her their names had represented nothing in her mind except unseen, unknown relatives to whom she was indebted for support, but to whom she also owed what she hated and rebelled against, - her imprisonment in the convent. Why should she love them? Blood tells, however; and when Victorine found herself free, and face to face with the grandfather of whom she had so long heard and only once seen, and the Aunt Jeanne who had been described to her as the loving benefactress of her youth, she had a new and affectionate sentiment towards them. But she would at any minute have calmly sacrificed them both for the furtherance of her own interests; and the thoughts she was thinking while Willan Blaycke gazed at her so ardently this night were precisely as follows: -

"If I could only have a good chance at him, I could make him marry me. I see it in his face. I suppose I'd never see Aunt Jeanne again, or grandfather; but what of that? I'd play my cards better than Aunt Jeanne did, I know that much. Let me once get to be mistress of that stone house - " And the color grew deeper and deeper on Victorine's cheeks in the excitement of these reflections.

"Poor girl!" Willan Blaycke was thinking. "I must not gaze at her so constantly. The color in her cheeks betrays that I distress her." And the honest gentleman tried his best to look away and bear good part in conversation with his friend. It was a doubly good stroke on the part of the wily Victorine to take her place behind the elder man's chair. It looked like a proper and modest preference on her part for age; and it kept her out of the old man's sight, and in the direct range of Willan's eyes as he conversed with his friend. When she had occasion to hand anything to Willan she did so with an apparent shyness which was captivating; and the tone of voice in which she spoke to him was low and timid.

Old Victor could hardly contain himself. He went back and forth between the dining-room and kitchen far oftener than was necessary, that he might have the pleasure of saying to Jeanne: "It works! it works! He doth gaze the eyes out of his head at her. The girl could not do better. She hath affected the very thing which will snare him the quickest."

"Oh no, father! Thou mistakest Victorine. She hath no plan of snaring him; it was with much ado I got her to consent to serve him at all. It was but for my sake she did it."

Victor stared at Jeanne when she said this. "Thou hast not told her, then?" he said.

"Nay, that would have spoiled all; if the girl herself had it in her head, he would have seen it."

Victor walked slowly back into the dining-room, and took further and closer observations of Mademoiselle Victorine's behavior and expressions. When he went next to the kitchen he clapped Jeanne on the shoulder, and said with a laugh: "'Tis a wise mother knows her own child. If that girl in yonder be not bent on turning the head of Willan Blaycke before she sleeps to-night, may the devil fly away with me!"

"Well, likely he may, if thou prove not too heavy a load," retorted the filial Jeanne. "I tell thee the girl's heart is full of anger against Willan Blaycke. She is but doing my bidding. I charged her to see to it that he was pleased, that he should go away our friend."

"And so he will go," replied Victor, dryly; "but not for thy bidding or mine. The man is that far pleased already that he shifteth as if the very chair were hot beneath him. A most dutiful niece thou hast, Mistress Jeanne!"

When supper was over Willan Blaycke walked hastily out of the house. He wanted to be alone. The clouds had broken away, and the full moon shone out gloriously. The great pear-tree looked like a tree wrapped in cloud, its blossoms were so thick and white. Willan paced back and forth beneath it, where he had lain sleeping before supper. He looked toward the window from whence he had heard the singing voice. "It must have been she," he said. "How shall I bring it to pass to see her again? for that I will and must." He went to the window and looked in. All was dark. As he turned away the door at the farther end opened, and a ray of light flashing in from the hall beyond showed Victorine bearing in her hand the jug of cider. She had made this excuse to go to the storeroom again, having observed that Willan had left the house.

"He might seek me again there," thought she.

Willan heard the sound, turned back, and bounding to the window exclaimed, "Was it thou who sang?"

Victorine affected not to hear. Setting down her jug, she came close to the window and said respectfully: "Didst thou call? What can I fetch, sir?"

Willan Blaycke leaned both his arms on the window-sill, and looking into the eyes of Victorine Dubois replied: "Marry, girl, thou hast already fetched me to such a pass that thy voice rings in my ears. I asked thee if it were thou who sang?"

Retreating from the window a step or two, Victorine said sorrowfully: "I did not think that thou hadst the face of one who would jest lightly with maidens." And she made as if she would go away.

"Pardon, pardon!" cried Willan. "I am not jesting; I implore thee, think it not. I did sleep under this tree before supper, and heard such singing! I had thought it a bird over my head except that the song had words. I know it was thou. Be not angry. Why shouldst thou? Where didst thou learn those wild songs?"

"From Sister Clarice, in the convent," answered Victorine. "It is only last Easter that my grandfather fetched me from the convent to live with him and my aunt Jeanne."

"Thy aunt Jeanne," said Willan, slowly. "Is she thy aunt?"

"Yes," said Victorine, sadly; "she that was thy father's wife, whom thou wilt not have in thy house."

This was a bold stroke on Victorine's part. To tell truth, she had had no idea one moment before of saying any such thing; but a sudden emotion of resentment got the better of her, and the words were uttered before she knew it.

Willan was angry. "All alike," he thought to himself, - "a bad lot. I dare say the woman has set the girl here for nothing else than to try to play on my feelings." And it was in a very cold tone that he replied to Victorine, -

"Thou art not able to judge of such matters at thy age. Thy aunt is better here than there. Thou knowest," he added in a gentler tone, seeing Victorine's great black eyes swimming in sudden tears, "that she was never as mother to me. I had never seen her till I returned a man grown."

Victorine was sobbing now. "Oh," she cried, "what ill

Helen Hunt Jackson

luck is mine! I have angered thee; and my aunt did especially charge me that I was to treat thee well. She doth never speak an ill word of thee, sir, never! Do not thou charge my hasty words to her." And Victorine leaned out of the window, and looked up in Willan Blaycke's face with a look which she had had good reason to know was well calculated to move a man's heart.

Willan Blaycke had led a singularly pure life. He was of a reticent and partly phlegmatic nature; though he looked so like his father, he resembled him little in temperament. This calmness of nature, added to a deep-seated pride, had stood him in stead of firmly rooted principles of virtue, and had carried him safe through all the temptations of his unprotected and lonely youth. He had the air and bearing, and had had in most things the experience, of a man of the world; and yet he was as ignorant of the wily ways of a wily woman as if he had never been out of the wilderness. Victorine's tears smote on him poignantly.

"Thou poor child!" he said most kindly, "do not weep. Thou hast done no harm. I bear no ill will to thine aunt, and never did; and if I had, thou wouldst have disarmed it. This inn seems to me no place for a young maiden like thee."

Victorine glanced cautiously around her, and whispered: "It were ungrateful in me to say as much; but oh, sir, if thou didst but know how I wish myself back in the convent! I like not the ways of this place; and I fear so much the men who are often here. When thou didst speak at first I did think thou wert like them; but now I perceive that thou art quite different. Thou seemest to me like the men of whom Sister Clarice did tell me." Victorine stopped, called up a blush to her cheeks, and said: "But I must not stay talking with thee. My aunt will be looking for me."

"Stay," said Willan. "What did the Sister Clarice tell thee of men? I thought not that nuns conversed on such matters."

"Oh!" replied Victorine, innocently, "it was different with the Sister Clarice. She was a noble lady who had been betrothed, and her betrothed died; and it was because there were none left so noble and so good as he, she said, that she had taken the veil and would die in the convent. She did talk to me whole nights about this young lord whom she was to have wed, and she did think often that she saw his face look down through the roof of the cell."

Clever Victorine! She had invented this tale on the spur of the instant. She could not have done better if she had plotted long to devise a method of flattering Willan Blaycke. It is strange how like inspiration are the impulses of artful women at times. It would seem wellnigh certain that they must be prompted by malicious fiends wishing to lure men on to destruction in the surest way.

Victorine had talked with Willan perhaps five minutes. In that space of time she had persuaded him of four things, all false, - that she was an innocent, guileless girl; that she had been seized with a sudden and reverential admiration for him; that she had no greater desire in life than to be back again in the safe shelter of the convent; and that her aunt Jeanne had never said an ill-word of him.

"Victorine! Victorine!" called a sharp loud voice, - the voice of Jeanne, - who would have bitten her tongue out rather than have broken in on this interview, if she had only known. "Victorine, where art thou loitering?"

"Oh, for heaven's sake, sir, do not thou tell my grandfather that I have talked with thee!" cried Victorine, in feigned terror. "Here I am, aunt; I will be there in one second," she cried aloud, and ran hastily down the storeroom. At the door she stopped, hesitated, turned back, and going towards the window said wistfully: "Thou hast never been here before all these three months. I suppose thou travellest this way very seldom."

The full moon shone on Victorine's face as she said this. Her expression was like that of a wistful little child. Willan Blaycke did not quite know what he was doing. He reached his hand across the window-sill towards Victorine; she did not extend hers. "I will come again sooner," he said. "Wilt thou not shake hands?"

Victorine advanced, hesitated, advanced again; it was inimitably done. "The next time, if I know thee better, I might dare," she whispered, and fled like a deer.

"Where hast thou been?" said Jeanne, angrily. "The supper dishes are yet all to wash."

Victorine danced gayly around the kitchen floor. "Talking with the son of thy husband," she said. "He seems to me much cleverer than a magpie."

Jeanne burst out laughing. "Thou witch!" she said, secretly well pleased. "But where didst thou fall upon him? Thou hast not been in the bar-room?"

"Nay, he fell upon me, the rather," replied Victorine, artlessly, "as I was resting me at the window of the long storeroom. He heard me singing, and came there."

"Did he praise thy voice?" asked Jeanne. "He is a brave singer himself."

"Is he?" said Victorine, eagerly. "He did not tell me that. He said my voice was like the voice of a wild bird. And there be birds and birds again, I was minded to tell him, and not all birds make music; but he seemed to me not one to take jests readily."

"So," said Jeanne; "that he is not. Leaves he early in the morning?"

"I think so," replied Victorine. "He did not tell me, but I heard the elder man say to Benoit to have the horses ready at earliest light."

"Thou must serve them again in the morning," said Jeanne. "It will be but the once more."

"Nay," answered Victorine, "I will not."

Something in the girl's tone arrested her aunt's attention. "And why?" she said sharply, looking scrutinizingly at her.

Victorine returned the gaze with one as steady. It was as well, she thought, that there should be an understanding between her aunt and herself soon as late.

"Because he will come again the sooner, Aunt Jeanne,

if he sees me no more after to-night." And Victorine gave a little mocking nod with her head, turned towards the dresser piled high with dishes, and began to make a great clatter washing them.

Jeanne was silent. She did not know how to take this.

Victorine glanced up at her mischievously, and laughed aloud. "Better a grape for me than two figs for thee. Dost know the old proverb, Aunt Jeanne? Thou hadst thy figs; I will e'en pluck the grape."

"Bah, child! thou talkest wildly," said Jeanne; "I know not what thou 'rt at."

But she did know very well; only she did not choose to seem to understand. However, as she thought matters over later in the evening, in the solitude of her own room, one thing was clear to her, and that was that it would probably be safe to trust Mademoiselle Victorine to row her own boat; and Jeanne said as much to her father when he inquired of her how matters had sped.

In spite of Victorine's refusal to serve at the breakfast, she had not the least idea of letting Willan go away in the morning without being reminded of her presence. She was up before light, dressed in a pretty pink and white flowered gown, which set off her black hair and eyes well, and made her look as if she were related to an apple-blossom. She watched and listened till she heard the sound of voices and the horses' feet in the courtyard below; then throwing open her casement she leaned out and began to water her flowers on the stairway roof. At the first sound Willan Blaycke looked up and saw her. It was as pretty a picture as a man need wish to see, and Willan gazed his fill at it. The window was so high up in the air that the girl might well be supposed not to see anything which was going on in the courtyard; indeed, she never once looked that way, but went on daintily watering plant after plant, picking off dead leaves, crumpling them up in her fingers and throwing them down as if she were alone in the place; singing, too, softly in a low tone snatches of a song, the words of which went floating away tantalizingly over Willan's head, in spite of all his efforts to hear.

It was a great tribute to Victorine's powers as an actress that it never once crossed Willan's mind that she could possibly know he was looking at her all this time. It was equally a token of another man's estimate of her, that when old Benoit, hearing the singing, looked up and saw her watering her flowers at this unexampled hour, he said under his breath, "Diable!" and then glancing at the face of Willan, who stood gazing up at the window utterly unconscious of the old ostler's presence, said "Diable!" again, but this time with a broad and amused smile.

III.

The fountain leaps as if its nearest goal
Were sky, and shines as if its life were light.
No crystal prism flashes on our sight
Such radiant splendor of the rainbow's whole
Of color. Who would dream the fountain stole
Its tints, and if the sun no more were bright
Would instant fade to its own pallid white?
Who dream that never higher than the dole
Of its own source, its stream may rise?
　　Thus we
See often hearts of men that by love's glow
Are sudden lighted, lifted till they show
All semblances of true nobility;
The passion spent, they tire of purity,
And sink again to their own levels low!

The next time Willan Blaycke came to the Golden Pear
he did not see Victorine. This was by no device of
hers, though if she had considered beforehand she
could not better have helped on the impression she had
made on him than by letting him go away disappointed, having come hoping to see her. She was away
on a visit at the home of Pierre Gaspard the miller,
whose eldest daughter Annette was Victorine's one
friend in the parish. There was an eldest son, also,
Pierre second, on whom Mademoiselle Victorine had
cast observant glances, and had already thought to
herself that "if nothing else turned up - but there was
time enough yet." Not so thought Pierre, who was
madly in love with Victorine, and was so put about by
her cold and capricious ways with him that he was fast
coming to be good for nothing in the mill or on the

farm. But he is of no consequence in this account of the career of Mademoiselle, only this, - that if it had not been for him she had not probably been away from the Golden Pear on the occasion of Willan Blaycke's second visit. Pierre had not shown himself at the inn for some weeks, and Victorine was uneasy about him. Spite of her plans about a much finer bird in the bush, she was by no means minded to lose the bird she had in hand. She was too clear-sighted a young lady not to perceive that it would be no bad thing to be ultimately Mistress Gaspard of the mill, - no bad thing if she could not do better, of which she was as yet far from sure. So she had inveigled her aunt into taking the notion into her head that she needed change, and the two had ridden over to Gaspard's for a three days' visit, the very day before Willan arrived.

"I warrant me he was set aback when I did tell him as he alighted that I feared me he would not be well served just at present, as there was no woman about the house," said Victor, chuckling as he told Jeanne the story. "He did give a little start, - not so little but that I saw it well, though he fetched himself up with his pride in a trice, and said loftily: 'I have no doubt all will be sufficient; it is but a bite of supper and a bed that I require. I must go on at daybreak,' But Benoit saw him all the evening pacing back and forth under the pear-tree, and many times looking up at the shut casement of the window where he had seen Victorine standing on the morning when he was last here."

"Did he ask aught about her?" said Jeanne.

"Bah!" said Victor, contemptuously. "Dost take him for a fool? He will be farther gone than he is yet, ere he will let either thee or me see that the girl is aught to him."

"I wish he had found her here," said Jeanne. "It was an ill bit of luck that took her away; and that Pierre, he is like to go mad about her, since these three days under one roof. I knew not he was so daft, or I had not taken her there."

"She were well wed to Pierre Gaspard," said Victor; "mated with one's own degree is best mated, after all. What shall we say if the lad come asking her hand? He will not ask twice, I can tell you that of a Gaspard."

"Trust the girl to keep him from asking till she be ready to say him yea or nay," replied Jeanne. "I know not wherever the child hath learnt such ways with men; surely in the convent she saw none but priests."

"And are not priests men?" sneered Victor, with an evil laugh. "Faith, and I think there is nought which other men teach which they do not teach better!"

"Fie, father! thou shouldst not speak ill of the clergy; it is bad luck," said Jeanne. Jeanne was far honester of nature than either her father or her child; she was not entirely without reverence, and as far as she could, without too much inconvenience, kept good faith with her religion.

When Victorine heard that Willan Blaycke had been at the inn in their absence, she shrugged her pretty shoulders, and said, laughingly, "Eh, but that is good!"

"Why sayest thou so?" replied Jeanne. "I say it is ill."

"And I say it is good," retorted Victorine; and not

another word could Jeanne get out of her on the matter.

Victorine was right. As Willan Blaycke rode away from the Golden Pear, he was so vexed with the unexpected disappointment that he was in a mood fit to do some desperate thing. He had tried with all his might to put Victorine's face and voice and sweet little form out of his thoughts, but it was beyond his power. She haunted him by day and by night, - worse by night than by day, - for he dreamed continually of standing just the other side of a window-sill across which Victorine reached snowy little hands and laid them in his, and just as he was about to grasp them the vision faded, and he waked up to find himself alone. Willan Blaycke had never loved any woman. If he had, - if he had had even the least experience in the way of passionate fancies, he could have rated this impression which Victorine had produced on him for what it was worth and no more, and taking counsel of his pride have waited till the discomfort of it should have passed away. But he knew no better than to suppose that because it was so keen, so haunting, it must last forever. He was almost appalled at the condition in which he found himself. It more than equalled all the descriptions which he had read of unquenchable love. He could not eat; he could not occupy himself with any affairs: all business was tedious to him, and all society irksome. He lay awake long hours, seeing the arch black eyes and rosy cheeks and piquant little mouth; worn out by restlessness, he slept, only to see the eyes and cheeks and mouth more vividly. It was all to no purpose that he reasoned with himself, - that he asked himself sternly a hundred times a day, -

"Wilt thou take the granddaughter of Victor Dubois to be the mother of thy children? Is it not enough that thy father disgraced his name for that blood? Wilt thou do likewise?"

The only answer which came to all these questions was Victorine's soft whisper: "Oh, if thou didst but know, sir, how I wish myself safe back in the convent!" and, "Thou seemest to me like the men of whom Sister Clarice did tell me."

"Poor little girl!" he said; "she is of their blood, but not of their sort. Her mother was doubtless a good and pure woman, even though she had not good birth or breeding; and this child hath had good training from the Sisters in the convent. She is of a most ladylike bearing, and has a fine sense of all which is proper and becoming, else would she not so dislike the ways of an inn, and have such fear of the men that gaze on her there."

So touching is the blindness of those blinded by love! It is enough to make one weep sometimes to see it, - to see, as in this instance of Willan Blaycke, an upright, modest, and honest gentleman creating out of the very virtues of his own nature the being whom he will worship, and then clothing this ideal with a bit of common clay, of immodest and ill-behaved flesh, which he hath found ready-made to his hand, and full of the snare of good looks.

When Willan Blaycke rode away this time from the Golden Pear, he was, as we say, in a mood ready to do some desperate thing, he was so vexed and disappointed. What he did do, proved it; he turned his horse and rode straight for Gaspard's mill. The artful Benoit had innocently dropped the remark, as he was holding the stirrup for Willan to mount, that Mistress

Jeanne and her niece were at Pierre Gaspard's; that for his part he wished them back, - there was no luck about a house without a woman in it.

Willan Blaycke made some indifferent reply, as if all that were nothing to him, and galloped off. But before he had gone five miles Benoit's leaven worked, and he turned into a short-cut lane he knew which led to the mill. He did not stop to ask himself what he should do there; he simply galloped on towards Victorine. It was only a couple of leagues to the mill, and its old tower and wheel were in sight before he thought of its being near. Then he began to consider what errand he could make; none occurred to him. He reined his horse up to a slow walk, and fell into a reverie, - so deep a one that he did not see what he might have seen had he looked attentively into a copse of poplars on a high bank close to his road, - two young girls sitting on the ground peeling slender willow stems for baskets. It was Annette Gaspard and Victorine; and at the sound of a horse's feet they both leaned forward and looked down into the road.

"Oh, see, Victorine!" Annette cried; "a brave rider goes there. Who can he be? I wonder if he goes to the mill? Perhaps my father will keep him to dinner."

At the first glance Victorine recognized Willan Blaycke, but she gave no sign to her friend that she knew him.

"He sitteth his horse like one asleep," she said, "or in a dream. I call him not a brave rider. He hath forgotten something," she added; "see, he is turning about!" And with keen disappointment the girls saw the horseman wheel suddenly, and gallop back on the road he had come. At the last moment, by a mighty effort, Willan had wrenched his will to the decision that he would not seek Victorine at the mill.

And this was why, when her aunt told her that he had been at the inn during their absence, Victorine shrugged her shoulders, and said with so pleased a laugh, "Eh! that is good." She understood by a lightning intuition all which had happened, - that he had ridden towards the mill seeking her, and had changed his mind at the last, and gone away. But she kept her own counsel, told nobody that she had seen him, and said in her mischievous heart, "He will be back before long."

And so he was; but not even Victorine, with all her confidence in the strength of the hold she had so suddenly acquired on him, could have imagined how soon and with what purpose he would return. On the evening of the sixth day, just at sunset, he appeared, walking with his saddle-bags on his shoulders and leading his horse. The beast limped badly, and had evidently got a sore hurt. Old Benoit was standing in the arched entrance of the courtyard as they approached.

"Marry, but that beast is in a bad way!" he exclaimed, and went to meet them. Benoit loved a horse; and Willan Blaycke's black stallion was a horse to which any man's heart might well go out, so knowing, docile, proud, and swift was the creature, and withal most beautifully made. The poor thing went haltingly enough now, and every few minutes stopped and looked around piteously into his master's face.

"And the man doth look as distressed as the beast,"

thought Benoit, as he drew near; "it is a good man that so loves an animal." And Benoit warmed toward Willan as he saw his anxious face.

If Benoit had only known! No wonder Willan's face was sorrow-stricken! It was he himself that had purposely lamed the stallion, that he might have plain and reasonable excuse for staying at the Golden Pear some days. He had not meant to hurt the poor creature so much, and his conscience pricked him horribly at every step the horse took. He patted him on his neck, spoke kindly to him, and did all in his power to atone for his cruelty. That all was very little, however, for each step was torture to the beast; his fore feet were nearly bleeding. This was what Willan had done: the day before he had taken off two of the horse's shoes, and then galloped fast over miles of rough and stony road. The horse had borne himself gallantly, and shown no fatigue till nightfall, when he suddenly went lame, and had grown worse in the night, so that Willan had come very near having to lie by at an inn some leagues to the north, where he had no mind to stay. A heavy price he was paying for the delight of looking on Victorine's face, he began to think, as he toiled along on foot, mile after mile, the saddle-bags on his shoulders, and the hot sun beating down on his head; but reach the Golden Pear that day he would, and he did, - almost as footsore as the stallion. Neither master nor beast was wonted to rough ways.

"My horse is sadly lame," Willan said to Benoit as he came up. "He cast two shoes yesterday, and I was forced to ride on, spite of it, for there was no black-smith on the road I came. I fear me thou canst not shoe him to-night, his feet have grown so sore!"

"No, nor to-morrow nor the day after," cried Benoit, taking up the inflamed feet and looking at them closely. "It was a sin, sir, to ride such a creature unshod; he is a noble steed."

"Nay, I have not ridden a step to-day," answered Willan, "and I am wellnigh as sore as he. We have come all the way from the north boundary, - a matter of some six leagues, I think, - from the inn of Jean Gauvois."

"But he is a farrier himself!" cried Benoit. "How let he the beast go out like this?"

"It was I forbade him to touch the horse," replied the wily Willan. "He did lame a good mare for me once, driving a nail into the quick. I thought the horse would be better to walk this far and get thy more skilful handling. There is not a man in this country, they tell me, can shoe a horse so well as thou. Dost thou not know some secret of healing," he continued, "by which thou canst harden the feet, so that they will be fit to shoe to-morrow?"

Benoit shook his head. "Thy horse hath been too tenderly reared," he said. "A hurt goes harder with him than with our horses. But I will do my best, sir. I doubt not it will inconvenience thee much to wait here till he be well. If thou couldst content thee with a beast sorry to look at, but like the wind to go, we have a nag would carry thee along, and thou couldst leave the stallion till thy return."

"But I come not back this way," replied Willan, strangely ready with his lies, now he had once undertaken the rôle of a manoeuvrer. "I go far south, even down to the harbors of the sound. I must bide the beast's time now. He hath made time for me many a day, and I do assure you, good Benoit, I love him as if he were my brother."

"Ay," replied the ostler; "so thought I when I saw thee bent under thy saddle-bags and leading the horse by the rein. It's an evil man likes not his beast. We say in Normandy, sir, -

> "'Evil master to good beast,
> Serve him ill at every feast!'"

"So he deserves," replied Willan, heartily; and in his heart he added, "I hope I shall not get my deserts."

Benoit led the poor horse away toward the stables, and Willan entered the house. No one was to be seen. Benoit had forgotten to tell him that no one was at home except Victorine. It was a market-day at St. Urban's; and Victor and Jeanne had gone for the day, and would not be back till late in the evening.

Willan roamed on from room to room, - through the bar-room, the living-room, the kitchen; all were empty, silent. As he retraced his steps he stopped for a second at the foot of the stairs which led from the living-room to the narrow passage-way overhead.

Victorine was in her aunt's room, and heard the steps. "Who is there?" she called. Willan recognized her voice; he considered a second what he should reply.

"Benoit! is it thou?" Victorine called again impatiently; and the next minute she bounded down the stairway, crying, "Why dost thou terrify me so, thou bad Benoit,

Helen Hunt Jackson

not answering me when I - " She stopped, face to face with Willan Blaycke, and gave a cry of honest surprise.

"Ah! but is it really thou?" she said, the rosy color mounting all over her face as she recollected how she was attired. She had been asleep all the warm afternoon, and had on only a white petticoat and a short gown of figured stuff, red and white. Her hair was falling over her shoulders. Willan's heart gave a bound as he looked at her. Before he had fairly seen her, she had turned to fly.

"Yes, it is I, - it is I," he called after her. "Wilt thou not come back?"

"Nay," answered Victorine, from the upper stair; "that I may not do, for the house is alone." Victorine was herself now, and was wise enough not to go quite out of sight. She looked entrancing between the dark wooden balustrades, one slender hand holding to them, and the other catching up part of her hair. "When my aunt returns, if she bids me to wait at supper I shall see thee." And Victorine was gone.

"Then sing for me at thy window," entreated Willan.

"I know not the whole of any song," cried Victorine; but broke, as she said it, into a snatch of a carol which seemed to the poor infatuated man at the foot of the stairway like the song of an angel. He hurried out, and threw himself down under the pear-tree where he had lain before. The blossoms had all fallen from the pear-tree now, and through the thinned branches he could see Victorine's window distinctly. She could see him also.

"It would be no hard thing to love such a man as he, methinks," she said to herself as she went on leisurely weaving the thick braids of her hair, and humming a song just low enough for Willan to half hear and half lose the words.

"Once in a hedge a bird went singing,
Singing because there was nobody near.
Close to the hedge a voice came crying,
'Sing it again! I am waiting to hear.
Sing it forever! 'T is sweet to hear.'

"Never again that bird went singing
Till it was surer that no one was near.
Long in that hedge there was somebody waiting,
Crying in vain, 'I am waiting to hear.
Sing it again! It was sweet to hear.'"

"I wonder if Sister Clarice's lover had asked her to sing, as Willan Blaycke just now asked me, that she did make this song," thought Victorine. "It hath a marvellous fitness, surely." And she repeated the last three lines.

"Long in that hedge there was somebody waiting,
Crying in vain, 'I am waiting to hear.
Sing it again! It was sweet to hear.'"

"But I should be silent like the bird, and not sing," she reflected, and paused for a while. Willan listened patiently for a few moments. Then growing impatient, he picked up a handful of turf and flung it up at the window. Victorine laughed to herself as she heard it, but did not sing. Another soft thud against the casement; no reply from Victorine. Then in a moment more, in a rich deep voice, and a tune far sweeter than any Victorine had sung, came these words: -

"Faint and weary toiled a pilgrim,
Faint and weary of his load;
Sudden came a sweet bird winging
Glad and swift across his road.

"'Blessed songster!' cried the pilgrim,
'Where is now the load I bore?
I forget it in thy singing;
Hearing thee, I faint no more,'

"While he spoke the bird went winging
Higher still, and soared away;
'Cruel songster!' cried the pilgrim,
'Cruel songster not to stay!'

"Was the songster cruel? Never!
High above some other road
Glad and swift he still was singing,
Lightening other pilgrims' load!"

Victorine bent her head and listened intently to this song. It touched the best side of her nature.

"Indeed, that is a good song," she said to herself, "but it fitteth not my singing. I make choice for whom I sing; I am not minded so to give pleasure to all the world."

She racked her brains to recall some song which would be as pertinent a reply to Willan's song as his had been to hers; but she could think of none. She was vexed; for the romance of this conversing by means of songs pleased her mightily. At last, half in earnest and half in fun, she struck boldly into a measure on which she would hardly have ventured could she have seen the serious and tender expression on the face of her listener under the pear-tree. As Willan caught line after line of the rollicking measure, his countenance changed.

"An elfish mood is upon her," he thought. "She doth hold herself so safe in her chamber that she may venture on words she had not sung nearer at hand. She is not without mischief in her blood, no doubt." And Willan's own look began to grow less reverential and more eager as he listened.

> "The bee is a fool in the summer;
> He knows it when summer is flown:
> He might, for all good of his honey,
> As well have let flowers alone.
>
> "The butterfly, he is the wiser;
> He uses his wings when they 're grown;
> He takes his delight in the summer,
> And dies when the summer is done.
>
> "A heart is a weight in the bosom;
> A heart can be heavy as stone:
> Oh, what is the use of a lover?
> A maiden is better alone."

Victorine was a little frightened herself, as she sang this last stanza. However, she said to herself: "I will bear me so discreetly at supper that the man shall doubt his very ears if he have ever heard me sing such words or not. It is well to perplex a man. The more he be perplexed, the more he meditateth on thee; and the more he meditateth on thee, the more his desire will grow, if it have once taken root."

A very wise young lady in her generation was this graduate of a convent where no men save priests ever came!

Just as Victorine had sung the last verse of her song, she heard the sound of wheels and voices on the road. Victor and Jeanne were coming home. Willan heard the sounds also, and slowly arose from the ground and sauntered into the courtyard. He had an instinct that it would be better not to be seen under the pear-tree.

Great was the satisfaction of Victor and Jeanne when they found that Willan Blaycke was a guest in the inn; still greater when they learned that he would be kept there for at least two days by the lameness of his horse.

"Thou need'st not make great haste with the healing of the beast," said Victor to Benoit; "it might be a good turn to keep the man here for a space." And the master exchanged one significant glance with his man, and saw that he need say no more.

There was no such specific understanding between Jeanne and Victorine. From some perverse and roguish impulse the girl chose to take no counsel in this game she had begun to play; but each woman knew that the other comprehended the situation perfectly.

When Victorine came into the dining-room to serve Willan Blaycke's supper, she looked, to his eyes, prettier than ever. She wore the same white gown and black silk apron with crimson lace she had worn before. Her cheeks and her eyes were bright from the excitement of the serenading and counter-serenading in which she had been engaged. Her whole bearing was an inimitable blending of shyness and archness, tempered by almost reverential respect. Willan Blaycke would have been either more or less than mortal man if he had resisted it. He did not, - he succumbed then and there and utterly to his love for Victorine; and the next morning when breakfast was ready he electrified Victor Dubois by saying, with a not wholly successful attempt at jocularity, -

"Look you! your man tells me I am like to be kept here a matter of some three days or more, before my horse be fit to bear me. Now, it irks me to be the cause of so much trouble, seeing that I am the only traveller in the house. I pray you that I may sit down with you all at meal-times, as is your wont, and that you make no change in the manner of your living by reason of my being in the house. I shall be better pleased so."

There was about as much command as request in Willan's manner; and after some pretended hesitancy Victor yielded, only saying, by way of breaking down the last barrier, -

"My daughter hath desired not to see thee. I know not how she may take this request of thine; it seemeth but reasonable unto me, and it will be that saving of work for her. I think she may consent."

Nothing but her love for Victorine would have induced Jeanne to sit again at meat with her stepson, but for Victorine's sake Jeanne would have done much harder things; and indeed, after the first few moments of awkwardness had passed by, she found that she was much less uncomfortable in Willan's presence than she had anticipated.

Willan's own manner did much to bring this about. He

was so deeply in love with Victorine that it had already transformed his sentiments on most points, and on none more than in regard to Jeanne. He thought no better of her character than he had thought before; but he found himself frequently recollecting, as he had never done before, or at least had never done in a kindly way, that, after all, she had been his father's wife for ten years, and it would perhaps have been a more dignified thing in him to have attempted to make her continue in a style of living suitable to his father's name than to have relegated her, as he had done, to her original and lower social station.

Jeanne's behavior towards him was very judicious. Affection is the best teacher of tact in many an emergency in life; we see it every day among ignorant and untaught people.

Jeanne knew, or felt without knowing, that the less she appeared to be conscious of anything unusual or unpleasant in this resumption of familiar relations on the surface, between herself and Willan, the more free his mind would be to occupy itself with Victorine; and she acted accordingly. She never obtruded herself on his attention; she never betrayed any antagonism toward him, or any recollection of the former and different footing on which they had lived. A stranger sitting at the table would not have dreamed, from anything in her manner to him, that she had ever occupied any other position than that of the landlord's daughter and landlady of the inn.

A clear-sighted observer looking on at affairs in the Golden Pear for the next three days would have seen that all the energies of both Victor and Jeanne were bent to one end, - namely, leaving the coast clear for

Willan Blaycke to fall in love with Victorine. But all that Willan thought was that Victor and his daughter were far quieter and modester people than he had supposed, and seemed disposed to keep themselves to themselves in a most proper fashion. It never crossed his mind that there was anything odd in his finding Victorine so often and so long alone in the living-room; in the uniform disappearance of both Victor and Jeanne at an early hour in the evening. Willan was too much in love to wonder at or disapprove of anything which gave him an opportunity of talking with Victorine, or, still better, of looking at her.

What he liked best was silently to watch her as she moved about, doing her light duties in her own graceful way. He was not a voluble lover; he was still too much bewildered at his own condition. Moreover, he had not yet shaken himself free from the tormenting disapproval of his conscience; he lost sight of that very fast, however, as the days sped on. Victorine played her cards most admirably. She did not betray even by a look that she understood that he loved her; she showed towards him an open and honest admiration, and an eager interest in all that he said or did, - an almost affectionate good-will, too, in serving his every want, and trying to make the time of his detention pass pleasantly to him.

"It must be a sore trial, sir, for thee to be kept in a poor place like this so many days. Benoit says that he thinks not thy horse can go safely for yet some days," she said to Willan one morning. "Would it amuse thee to ride over to Pierre Gaspard's mill to-day? If thou couldst abide the gait of my grandfather's nag, I might go on my pony, and show thee the way. The river is high now, and it is a fair sight to see the white blossoms along the banks."

Cunning Victorine! She had all sorts of motives in this proposition. She thought it would be well to show Willan Blaycke to Pierre. "He may discover that there are other men beside himself in the world," she mused; and, "It would please me much to go riding up to the door for Annette to see with the same brave rider she did so admire;" and, "There are many ways to bring a man near one in riding through the woods." All these and many more similar musings lay hid behind the innocent look she lifted to Willan's face as she suggested the ride.

It was only the third morning of Willan's stay at the inn; but the time had been put to very good use. Already it had become natural to him to come and go with Victorine, - to stay where she was, to seek her if she were missing. Already he had learned the way up the outside staircase to the platform where she kept her flowers and sometimes sat. He was living in a dream, - going the way of all men, head-long, blindfold, into a life of which he knew and could know nothing.

"Indeed, and that is what I should like best of all things," he replied to Victorine. "Will thy aunt let thee go?"

"Why not?" asked Victorine, opening her eyes wide in astonishment. "I ride all over the parish on my pony alone."

"Stupid of me!" ejaculated Willan, inwardly: "as if these people could know any scruples about etiquette!"

"These people," as Willan contemptuously called them,

stood at the door of the inn, and watched him riding away with Victorine with hardly disguised exultation. Not till the riders were fairly out of sight did Victor venture to turn his face toward Jeanne's. Then, bursting into a loud laugh, he clapped Jeanne on the shoulder, and said: "We'll see thee grandmother of thy husband's grandchildren yet, Jeanne. Ha! ha!"

Jeanne flushed. She was not without a sense of shame. Her love for Victorine made her sensitive to the stain on her birth.

"Thinkest thou it could ever be known?" she asked anxiously.

"Never," replied her father, - "never; 'tis as safe as if we were all dead. And for that, the living are safer than the dead, if there be tight enough lock on their mouths."

"He doth seem to be as much in love as one need," said Jeanne.

"Ay," said Victor, "more than ever his father was with thee."

"Canst thou not let that alone?" said Jeanne, angrily. "Surely it is long enough gone by, and small profit came of it."

"Not so, not so, daughter," replied Victor, soothingly; "if we can but set the girl in thy shoes, thou didst not wear thine for nought, even though they pinched thee for a time."

"That they did," retorted Jeanne; "it gives me a cramp

now but to remember them."

Willan and Victorine galloped merrily along the river road. The woods were sweet with spring fragrances; great thickets of dogwood trees were white with flowers; mossy hillocks along the roadside were pink with the dainty bells of the Linnaea. The road was little more than a woodman's path, and curved now right, now left, in seeming caprice; now forded a stream, now came out into a cleared field, again plunged back into dense groves of larch and pine.

"Never knew I that the woods were so beautiful thus early in the year," said the honest Willan.

"Nor I, till to-day," said the artful Victorine, who knew well enough what Willan did not know himself.

"Dost thou ride here alone?" asked Willan. "It is a wild place for thee to be alone."

"If I came not alone, I could not come at all," replied Victorine, sorrowfully. "My grandfather is too busy, and my aunt likes not to ride except she must, on a market day or to go to church. No one but thou hast ever walked or ridden with me," she added in a low voice, sighing; "and now after two days or three thou wilt be gone."

Willan sighed also, but did not speak. The words, "I will always ride by thy side, Victorine," were on his lips, but he felt himself still withheld from speaking them.

The visit at the mill was unsatisfactory. The elder Gaspard was away, and young Pierre was curt and surly. The sight of Victorine riding familiarly, and with an evident joyous pride, by the side of one of the richest men in the country, and a young man at that, - and a young man, moreover, who looked and behaved as if he were in love with his companion, - how could the poor miller be expected to be cordial and unconstrained with such a sight before his eyes! Annette also was more overawed even than Victorine had desired she should be by the sight of the handsome stranger, - so overawed, and withal perhaps a little curious, that she was dumb and awkward; and as for *Mère* Gaspard, she never under any circumstances had a word to say. So the visit was very stupid, and everybody felt ill at ease, - especially Willan, who had lost his temper in the beginning at a speech of Pierre's to Victorine, which seemed to his jealous sense too familiar.

"I thought thou never wouldst take leave," he said ill-naturedly to Victorine, as they rode away.

Victorine turned towards him with an admirably counterfeited expression of surprise. "Oh, sir," she said, "I did think I ought to wait for thee to take leave. I was dying with the desire I had to be back in the woods again; and only when I could not bear it any longer, did I bethink me to say that my aunt expected us back to dinner."

Long they lingered on the river-banks on their way home. Even the plotting brain of Victorine was not insensible to the charm of the sky, the air, the budding foliage, and the myriads of blossoms. "Oh, sir," she said, "I think there never was such a day as this before!"

"I know there never was," replied Willan, looking at her with an expression which was key to his words. But the daughter of Jeanne Dubois was not to be wooed by any vague sentimentalisms. There was one sentence which she was intently waiting to hear Willan Blaycke speak. Anything short of that Mademoiselle Victorine was too innocent to comprehend.

"Sweet child!" thought Willan to himself, "she doth not know the speech of lovers. I mistrust that if I wooed her outright, she would be afraid."

It was long past noon when they reached the Golden Pear. Dinner had waited till the hungry Victor and Jeanne could wait no longer; but a very pretty and dainty little repast was ready for Willan and Victorine. As she sat opposite him at the table, so bright and beaming, her whole face full of pleasure, Willan leaned both his arms on the table and looked at her in silence for some minutes.

"Victorine!" he said. Victorine started. She was honestly very hungry, and had been so absorbed in eating her dinner she had not noticed Willan's look. She dropped her knife and sprang up.

"What is it, sir?" she said; "what shall I fetch?" Her instantaneous resumption of the serving-maid's relation to him jarred on Willan at that second indescribably, and shut down like a floodgate on the words he was about to speak.

"Nothing, nothing," said he. "I was only going to say that thou must sleep this afternoon; thou art tired."

"Nay, I am not tired," said Victorine, petulantly. "What

is a matter of six leagues of a morning? I could ride it again between this and sunset, and not be tired."

But she was tired, and she did sleep, though she had not meant to do so when she threw herself on her bed, a little later; she had meant only to rest herself for a few minutes, and then in a fresh toilette return to Willan. But she slept on and on until after sunset, and Willan wandered aimlessly about, wondering what had become of her. Jeanne saw him, but forebore to take any note of his uneasiness. She had looked in upon Victorine in her slumber, and was well content that it should be so.

"The girl will awake refreshed and rosy," thought Jeanne; "and it will do no harm, but rather good, if he have missed her sorely all the afternoon."

Supper was over, and the evening work all done when Victorine waked. It was dusk. Rubbing her eyes, she sprang up and went to the window. Jeanne heard her steps, and coming to the foot of the stairs called: "Thou need'st not to come down; all is done. What shall I bring thee to eat?"

"Why didst thou not waken me?" replied Victorine, petulantly; "I meant not to sleep."

"I thought the sleep was better," replied her aunt. "Thou didst look tired, and it suits no woman's looks to be tired."

Victorine was silent. She saw Willan walking up and down under the pear-tree. She leaned out of her window and moved one of the flower-pots. Willan looked up; in a second more he had bounded up the staircase, and eagerly said: "Art thou there? Wilt thou never come down?"

Victorine was uncertain in her own mind what was the best thing to do next; so she replied evasively: "Thou wert right, after all. I did not feel myself tired, but I have slept until now."

"Then thou art surely rested. Canst thou not come and walk with me in the pear orchard?" said Willan.

"I fear me I may not do that after nightfall," replied Victorine. "My aunt would be angry."

"She need not know," replied the eager Willan. "Thou canst come down by this stairway, and it is already near dark."

Victorine laughed a little low laugh. This pleased her. "Yes," she said, "I have often come down by, that post from my window; but truly, I fear I ought not to do it for thee. What should I say to my aunt if she missed me?"

"Oh, she thinks thee asleep," said Willan. "She told me at supper that she would not waken thee."

All of which Mistress Jeanne heard distinctly, standing midway on the wide staircase, with Victorine's supper of bread and milk in her hand. She had like to have spilled the whole bowlful of milk for laughing. But she stood still, holding her breath lest Victorine should hear her, till the conversation ceased, and she heard Victorine moving about in her room again. Then she went in, and kissing Victorine, said: "Eat thy supper now, and go to bed; it is late. Good-night. I'll wake thee early enough in the morning to pay for not having called thee this afternoon. Good-night."

Then Jeanne went down to her own room, blew out her candle, and seated herself at the window to hear what would happen.

"My aunt's candle is out; she hath gone to bed," whispered Victorine, as holding Willan's hand she stole softly down the outer stair. "I do doubt much that I am doing wrong."

"Nay, nay," whispered Willan. "Thou sweet one, what wrong can there be in thy walking a little time with me? Thy aunt did let thee ride with me all the day." And he tenderly guided Victorine's steps down the steep stairs.

"Pretty well! pretty well!" laughed Mistress Jeanne behind her casement; and as soon as the sound of Willan's and Victorine's steps had died away, she ran downstairs to tell Victor what had happened. Victor was not so pleased as Jeanne; he did not share her confidence in Victorine's character.

"Sacre!" he said; "what wert thou thinking of? Dost want another niece to be fetched up in a convent? Thou mayst thank thyself for it, if thou art grandmother to one. I trust no man out of sight, and no girl. The man's in love with the girl, that is plain; but he means no marrying."

"That thou dost not know," retorted Jeanne. "I tell thee he is an honorable, high-minded man, and as pure as if he were but just now weaned. I know him, and thou dost not. He will marry her, or he will leave her alone."

"We shall see," muttered the coarse old man as he walked away, - "we shall see. Like mother, like child. I trust them not." And in a thorough ill-humor Victor betook himself to the courtyard. What he heard there did not reassure him. Old Benoit had seen Willan and Victorine going down through the poplar copse toward the pear orchard. "And may the saints forsake me," said Benoit, "if I do not think he had his arm around her waist and her head on his shoulder. Think'st thou he will marry her?"

"Nay," growled Victor; "he's no fool. That Jeanne hath set her heart on it, and thinketh it will come about; but not so I."

"He seems of a rare fine-breeding and honorable speech," said Benoit.

"Ay, ay," replied Victor, "words are quick said, and fine manners come easy to some; but a man looks where he weds."

"His father did not have chance for much looking," sneered Benoit.

"This is another breed, even if his father begot him," replied Victor. "He goeth no such way as that." And thoroughly disquieted, Victor returned to the house to report to Jeanne what Benoit had seen. She was still undisturbed.

"Thou wilt see," was her only reply; and the two sat down together in the porch to await the lovers' return. Hour after hour passed; even Jeanne began to grow alarmed. It was long after midnight.

"I fear some accident hath befallen them," she said at last. "Would it be well, thinkest thou, to go in search of them?"

"Not a step!" cried Victor. "He took her away, and he must needs bring her back. We await them here. He shall see whether he may tamper with the grand-daughter of Victor Dubois."

"Hush, father!" said Jeanne, "here they come."

Walking very slowly, arm in arm, came Willan and Victorine. They had evidently no purpose of entering the house clandestinely, but were approaching the front door.

"Hoity, toity!" muttered Victor; "he thinks he can lord it over us, surely."

"Be quiet, father!" entreated Jeanne. Her quick eye saw something new in the bearing of both Willan and Victorine. But Victor was not to be quieted. With an angry oath, he sprung forward from the porch, and began to upbraid Willan in no measured tones.

Willan lifted his right hand authoritatively. "Wait!" he said. "Do not say what thou wilt repent, Victor Dubois. Thy granddaughter hath promised to be my wife."

So the new generation avenged the old; and Willan Blaycke, in the prime of his cultured and fastidious manhood, fell victim to a spell less coarsely woven but no less demoralizing than that which had imbittered the last years of his father's life.

[Footnote: Note. - "The Inn of the Golden Pear"

includes three chapters of a longer story entitled "Elspeth Pynevor," - a story of such remarkable vigor and promise, and planned on such noble and powerful lines as to deepen regret that its author's death left it but half finished. A single sentence has been added by another hand to round the episode of Willan Blaycke's infatuation to conclusion.]

The Mystery of Wilhelm Rütter.

It was long past dusk of an August evening. Farmer Weitbreck stood leaning on the big gate of his barnyard, looking first up and then down the road. He was chewing a straw, and his face wore an expression of deep perplexity. These were troublous times in Lancaster County. Never before had the farmers been so put to it for farm service; harvest-time had come, and instead of the stream of laborers seeking employment, which usually at this season set in as regularly as river freshets in spring, it was this year almost impossible to hire any one.

The explanation of this nobody knew or could divine; but the fact was indisputable, and the farmers were in dismay, - nobody more so than Farmer Weitbreck, who had miles of bottom-lands, in grain of one sort and another, all yellow and nodding, and ready for the sickle, and nobody but himself and his son John to swing scythe, sickle, or flail on the place.

"Never I am caught this way anoder year," thought he, as he gazed wearily up and down the dark, silent road; "but that does to me no goot this time that is now."

Gustavus Weitbreck had lived so long on his Pennsylvania farm that he even thought in English instead of in German, and, strangely enough, in

English much less broken and idiomatic than that which he spoke. But his phraseology was the only thing about him that had changed. In modes of feeling, habits of life, he was the same he had been forty years ago, when he farmed a little plot of land, half wheat, half vineyard, in the Mayence meadows in the fatherland, - slow, methodical, saving, stupid, upright, obstinate. All these traits "Old Weitbreck," as he was called all through the country, possessed to a degree much out of the ordinary; and it was a combination of two of them - the obstinacy and the savingness - which had brought him into his present predicament.

In June he had had a good laborer, - one of the best known, and eagerly sought by every farmer in the county; a man who had never yet been beaten in a mowing-match or a reaping. By his help the haying had been done in not much more than two thirds the usual time; but when John Weitbreck, like a sensible fellow, said, "Now, we would better keep Alf on till harvest; there is plenty of odds-and-ends work about the farm he can help at, and we won't get his like again in a hurry," his father had cried out, -

"Mein Gott! It is that you tink I must be made out of money! I vill not keep dis man on so big wages to do vat you call odd-and-end vork. We do odd-and-end vork ourself."

There was no discussion of the point. John Weitbreck knew better than ever to waste his time and breath or temper in trying to change a purpose of his father's or convince him of a mistake. But he bided his time; and he would not have been human if he had not now taken secret satisfaction, seeing his father's anxiety daily increase as the August sun grew hotter and hotter, and the grain rattled in the husks waiting to be reaped, while they two, straining their arms to the utmost, and in long days' work, seemed to produce small impression on the great fields.

"The women shall come work in field to-morrow," thought the old man, as he continued his anxious reverie. "It is not that they sit idle all day in house, when the wheat grows to rattle like the peas in pod. They can help, the mütter and Carlen; that will be much help; they can do." And hearing John's steps behind him, the old man turned and said, -

"Johan, dere comes yet no man to reap. To-morrow must go in the field Carlen and the mütter; it must. The wheat get fast too dry; it is more as two men can do."

John bit his lips. He was aghast. Never had he seen his mother and sister at work in the fields. John had been born in America; and he was American, not German, in his feeling about this. Without due consideration he answered, -

"I would rather work day and night, father, than see my mother and sister in the fields. I will do it, too, if only you will not make them go!"

The old man, irritated by the secret knowledge that he had nobody but himself to blame for the present dilemma, still more irritated, also, by this proof of what was always exceedingly displeasing to him, - his son's having adopted American standards and opinions, - broke out furiously with a wrath wholly disproportionate to the occasion, -

"You be tam, Johan Weitbreck. You tink we are fine

gentlemen and ladies, like dese Americans dat is too proud to vork vid hands. I say tam dis country, vere day say all is alike, an' vork all; and ven you come here, it is dat nobody vill vork, if he can help, and vimmins ish shame to be seen vork. It is not shame to be seen vork; I vork, mein vife vork too, an' my childrens vork too, py tam!"

John walked away, - his only resource when his father was in a passion. John occupied that hardest of all positions, - the position of a full-grown, mature man in a father's home, where he is regarded as nothing more than a boy.

As he entered the kitchen and saw his pretty sister Carlen at the high spinning-wheel, walking back and forth drawing the fine yarn between her chubby fingers, all the while humming a low song to which the whirring of the wheel made harmonious accompaniment, he thought to himself bitterly: "Work, indeed! As if they did not work now longer than we do, and quite as hard! She's been spinning ever since daylight, I believe."

"Is it hard work spinning, Liebchen?" he asked.

Carlen turned her round blue eyes on him with astonishment. There was something in his tone that smote vaguely on her consciousness. What could he mean, asking such a question as that?

"No," she said, "it is not hard exactly. But when you do it very long it does make the arms ache, holding them so long in the same position; and it tires one to stand all day!"

"Ay," said John, "that is the way it tires one to reap; my back is near broke with it to-day."

"Has no one come to help yet?" she said.

"No!" said John, angrily, "and that is what I told father when he let Alf go. It is good enough for him for being so stingy and short-sighted; but the brunt of it comes on me, - that's the worst of it. I don't see what's got all the men. There have always been plenty round every year till now."

"Alf said he shouldn't be here next year," said Carlen, each cheek showing a little signal of pink as she spoke; but it was a dim light the one candle gave, and John did not see the flush. "He was going to the west to farm; in Oregon, he said."

"Ay, that's it!" replied John. "That's where everybody can go but me! I'll be going too some day, Carlen. I can't stand things here. If it weren't for you I'd have been gone long ago."

"I wouldn't leave mother and father for all the world, John," cried Carlen, warmly, "and I don't think it would be right for you to! What would father do with the farm without you?"

"Well, why doesn't he see that, then, and treat me as a man ought to be treated?" exclaimed John; "he thinks I'm no older than when he used to beat me with the strap."

"I think fathers and mothers are always that way," said the gentle, cheery Carlen, with a low laugh. "The mother tells me each time how to wind the warp, as

Helen Hunt Jackson

she did when I was little; and she will always look into the churn for herself. I think it is the way we are made. We will do the same when we are old, John, and our children will be wondering at us!"

John laughed. This was always the way with Carlen. She could put a man in good humor in a few minutes, however cross he felt in the beginning.

"I won't, then!" he exclaimed. "I know I won't. If ever I have a son grown, I'll treat him like a son grown, not like a baby."

"May I be there to see!" said Carlen, merrily, -

"And you remember free
The words I said to thee.

"Hold the candle here for me, will you, that's a good boy. While we have talked, my yarn has tangled."

As they stood close together, John holding the candle high over Carlen's head, she bending over the tangled yarn, the kitchen door opened suddenly, and their father came in, bringing with him a stranger, - a young man seemingly about twenty-five years of age, tall, well made, handsome, but with a face so melancholy that both John and Carlen felt a shiver as they looked upon it.

"Here now comes de hand, at last of de time, Johan," cried the old man. "It vill be that all can vel be done now. And it is goot that he is from mine own country. He cannot English speak, many vords; but dat is nothing; he can vork. I tolt you dere vould be mans come!"

John looked scrutinizingly at the newcomer. The man's eyes fell.

"What is your name?" said John.

"Wilhelm Rütter," he answered.

"How long have you been in this country?"

"Ten days."

"Where are your friends?"

"I haf none."

"None?"

"None."

These replies were given in a tone as melancholy as the expression of the face.

Carlen stood still, her wheel arrested, the yarn between her thumb and ringer, her eyes fastened on the stranger's face. A thrill of unspeakable pity stirred her. So young, so sad, thus alone in the world; who ever heard of such a fate?

"But there were people who came with you in the ship?" said John. "There is some one who knows who you are, I suppose."

"No, no von dat knows," replied the newcomer.

"Haf done vid too much questions," interrupted Farmer Weitbreck. "I haf him asked all. He stays till harvest be done. He can vork. It is to be easy see he can vork."

John did not like the appearance of things. "Too much mystery here," he thought. "However, it is not long he will be here, and he will be in the fields all the time; there cannot be much danger. But who ever heard of a man whom no human being knew?"

As they sat at supper, Farmer Weitbreck and his wife plied Wilhelm with questions about their old friends in Mayence. He was evidently familiar with all the localities and names which they mentioned. His replies, however, were given as far as possible in monosyllables, and he spoke no word voluntarily. Sitting with his head bent slightly forward, his eyes fixed on the floor, he had the expression of one lost in thoughts of the gloomiest kind.

"Make yourself to be more happy, mein lad," said the farmer, as he bade him good-night and clapped him on the shoulder. "You haf come to house vere is German be speaked, and is Germany in hearts; dat vill be to you as friends."

A strange look of even keener pain passed over the young man's face, and he left the room hastily, without a word of good-night.

"He's a surly brute!" cried John; "nice company he'll be in the field! I believe I'd sooner have nobody!"

"I think he has seen some dreadful trouble," said Carlen. "I wish we could do something for him; perhaps his friends are all dead. I think that must be it, don't you think so, mütter?"

Frau Weitbreck was incarnate silence and reticence. These traits were native in her, and had been intensified to an abnormal extent by thirty years of life with a husband whose temper and peculiarities were such as to make silence and reticence the sole conditions of peace and comfort. To so great a degree had this second nature of the good frau been developed, that she herself did not now know that it was a second nature; therefore it stood her in hand as well as if she had been originally born to it, and it would have been hard to find in Lancaster County a more placid and contented wife than she. She never dreamed that her custom of silent acquiescence in all that Gustavus said - of waiting in all cases, small and great, for his decision - had in the outset been born of radical and uncomfortable disagreements with him. And as for Gustavus himself, if anybody had hinted to him that his frau could think, or ever had thought, any word or deed of his other than right, he would have chuckled complacently at that person's blind ignorance of the truth.

"Mein frau, she is goot," he said; "goot frau, goot mütter. American fraus not goot so she; all de time talk and no vork. American fraus, American mans, are sheep in dere house."

But in regard to this young stranger, Frau Weitbreck seemed strangely stirred from her usual phlegmatic silence. Carlen's appeal to her had barely been spoken, when, rising in her place at the head of the table, the old woman said solemnly, in German, -

"Yes, Liebchen, he goes with the eyes like eyes of a man that saw always the dead. It must be as you say, that all whom he loves are in the grave. Poor boy! poor boy! it is now that one must be to him mother and father and brother."

"And sister too," said Carlen, warmly. "I will be his sister."

"And I not his brother till he gets a civiller tongue in his head," said John.

"It is not to be brother I haf him brought," interrupted the old man. "Alvays you vimmen are too soon; it may be he are goot, it may be he are pad; I do not know. It is to vork I haf him brought."

"Yes," echoed Frau Weitbreck; "we do not know."

It was not so easy as Carlen and her mother had thought, to be like mother and sister to Wilhelm. The days went by, and still he was as much a stranger as on the evening of his arrival. He never voluntarily addressed any one. To all remarks or even questions he replied in the fewest words and curtest phrases possible. A smile was never seen on his face. He sat at the table like a mute at a funeral, ate without lifting his eyes, and silently rose as soon as his own meal was finished. He had soon selected his favorite seat in the kitchen. It was on the right-hand side of the big fireplace, in a corner. Here he sat all through the evenings, carving, out of cows' horns or wood, boxes and small figures such as are made by the peasants in the German Tyrol. In this work he had a surprising skill. What he did with the carvings when finished, no one knew. One night John said to him, -

"I do not see, Wilhelm, how you can have so steady a hand after holding the sickle all day. My arm aches, and my hand trembles so that I can but just carry my cup to my lips."

Wilhelm made no reply, but held his right hand straight out at arm's length, with the delicate figure he was carving poised on his forefinger. It stood as steady as on the firm ground.

Carlen looked at him admiringly. "It is good to be so steady-handed," she said; "you must be strong, Wilhelm."

"Yes," he said, "I haf strong;" and went on carving.

Nothing more like conversation than this was ever drawn from him. Yet he seemed not averse to seeing people. He never left the kitchen till the time came for bed; but when that came he slipped away silent, taking no part in the general good-night unless he was forced to do so. Sometimes Carlen, having said jokingly to John, "Now, I will make Wilhelm say good-night to-night," succeeded in surprising him before he could leave the room; but often, even when she had thus planned, he contrived to evade her, and was gone before she knew it.

He slept in a small chamber in the barn, - a dreary enough little place, but he seemed to find it all sufficient. He had no possessions except the leather pack he had brought on his back. This lay on the floor unlocked; and when the good Frau Weitbreck, persuading herself that she was actuated solely by a righteous, motherly interest in the young man, opened it, she found nothing whatever there, except a few garments of the commonest description, - no book, no paper, no name on any article. It would not appear

Helen Hunt Jackson

possible that a man of so decent a seeming as Wilhelm could have come from Germany to America with so few personal belongings. Frau Weitbreck felt less at ease in her mind about him after she examined this pack.

He had come straight from the ship to their house, he had said, when he arrived; had walked on day after day, going he knew not whither, asking mile by mile for work. He did not even know one State's name from another. He simply chose to go south rather than north, - always south, he said.

"Why?"

He did not know.

He was indeed strong. The sickle was in his hand a plaything, so swift-swung that he seemed to be doing little more than simply striding up and down the field, the grain falling to right and left at his steps. From sunrise to sunset he worked tirelessly. The famous Alf had never done so much in a day. Farmer Weitbreck chuckled as he looked on.

"Vat now you say of dat Alf?" he said triumphantly to John; "vork he as dis man? Oh, but he make swing de hook!"

John assented unqualifiedly to this praise of Wilhelm's strength and skill; but nevertheless he shook his head.

"Ay, ay," he said, "I never saw his equal; but I like him not. What carries he in his heart to be so sour? He is like a man bewitched. I know not if there be such a thing as to be sold to the devil, as the stories say; but if there be, on my word, I think Wilhelm has made some such bargain. A man could not look worse if he had signed himself away."

"I see not dat he haf fear in his face," replied the old man.

"No," said John, "neither do I see fear. It is worse than fear. I would like to see his face come alive with a fear. He gives me cold shivers like a grave underfoot. I shall be glad when he is gone."

Farmer Weitbreck laughed. He and his son were likely to be again at odds on the subject of a laborer.

"But he vill not go. I haf said to him to stay till Christmas, maybe always."

John's surprise was unbounded.

"To stay! Till Christmas!" he cried. "What for? What do we need of a man in the winter?"

"It is not dat to feed him is much, and all dat he make vid de knife is mine. It is home he vants, no oder ting; he vork not for money."

"Father," said John, earnestly, "there must be something wrong about that man. I have thought so from the first. Why should he work for nothing but his board, - a great strong fellow like that, that could make good day's wages anywhere? Don't keep him after the harvest is over. I can't bear the sight of him."

"Den you can turn de eyes to your head von oder way," retorted his father. "I find him goot to see; and," after a pause, "so do Carlen."

John started. "Good heavens, father!" he exclaimed.

"Oh, you need not speak by de heavens, mein son!" rejoined the old man, in a taunting tone. "I tink I can mine own vay, vidout you to be help. I was not yesterday born!"

John was gone. Flight was his usual refuge when he felt his temper becoming too much for him; but now his steps were quickened by an impulse of terrible fear. Between him and his sister had always been a bond closer than is wont to link brother and sister. Only one year apart in age, they had grown up together in an intimacy like that of twins; from their cradles till now they had had their sports, tastes, joys, sorrows in common, not a secret from each other since they could remember. At least, this was true of John; was he to find it no longer true of Carlen? He would know, and that right speedily. As by a flash of lightning he thought he saw his father's scheme, - if Carlen were to wed this man, this strong and tireless worker, this unknown, mysterious worker, who wanted only shelter and home and cared not for money, what an invaluable hand would be gained on the farm! John groaned as he thought to himself how little anything - any doubt, any misgiving, perhaps even an actual danger - would in his father's mind outweigh the one fact that the man did not "vork for money."

As he walked toward the house, revolving these disquieting conjectures, all his first suspicion and antagonism toward Wilhelm revived in full force, and he was in a mood well calculated to distort the simplest acts, when he suddenly saw sitting in the square stoop at the door the two persons who filled his thoughts, Wilhelm and Carlen, - Wilhelm steadily at work as usual at his carving, his eyes closely fixed on it, his figure, as was its wont, rigidly still; and Carlen, - ah! it was an unlucky moment John had taken to search out the state of Carlen's feeling toward Wilhelm, - Carlen sitting in a posture of dreamy reverie, one hand lying idle in her lap holding her knitting, the ball rolling away unnoticed on the ground; her other arm thrown carelessly over the railing of the stoop, her eyes fixed on Wilhelm's bowed head.

John stood still and watched her, - watched her long. She did not move. She was almost as rigidly still as Wilhelm himself. Her eyes did not leave his face. One might safely sit in that way by the hour and gaze undetected at Wilhelm. He rarely looked up except when he was addressed.

After standing thus a few moments John turned away, bitter and sick at heart. What had he been about, that he had not seen this? He, the loving comrade brother, to be slower of sight than the hard, grasping parent!

"I will ask mother," he thought. "I can't ask Carlen now! It is too late."

He found his mother in the kitchen, busy getting the bountiful supper which was a daily ordinance in the Weitbreck religion. To John's sharpened perceptions the fact that Carlen was not as usual helping in this labor loomed up into significance.

"Why does not Carlen help you, mütter?" he said hastily. "What is she doing there, idling with Wilhelm in the stoop?"

Frau Weitbreck smiled. "It is not alvays to vork, ven one is young," she said. "I haf not forget!" And she nodded her head meaningly.

John clenched his hands. Where had he been? Who had blinded him? How had all this come about, so soon and without his knowledge? Were his father and his mother mad? He thought they must be.

"It is a shame for that Wilhelm to so much as put his eyes on Carlen's face," he cried. "I think we are fools; what know we about him? I doubt him in and out. I wish he had never darkened our doors."

Frau Weitbreck glanced cautiously at the open door. She was frying sweet cakes in the boiling lard. Forgetting everything in her fear of being overheard, she went softly, with the dripping skimmer in her hand, across the kitchen, the fat falling on her shining floor at every step, and closed the door. Then she came close to her son, and said in a whisper, "The fader think it is goot." At John's angry exclamation she raised her hand in warning.

"Do not loud spraken," she whispered; "Carlen will hear."

"Well, then, she shall hear!" cried John, half beside himself. "It is high time she did hear from somebody besides you and father! I reckon I've got something to say about this thing, too, if I'm her brother. By - , no tramp like that is going to marry my sister without I know more about him!" And before the terrified old woman could stop him, he had gone at long strides across the kitchen, through the best room, and reached the stoop, saying in a loud tone: "Carlen! I want to see you."

Carlen started as one roused from sleep. Seeing her ball lying at a distance on the ground, she ran to pick it up, and with scarlet cheeks and uneasy eyes turned to her brother.

"Yes, John," she said, "I am coming."

Wilhelm did not raise his eyes, or betray by any change of feature that he had heard the sound or perceived the motion. As Carlen passed him her eyes involuntarily rested on his bowed head, a world of pity, perplexity, in the glance. John saw it, and frowned.

"Come with me," he said sternly, - "come down in the pasture; I want to speak to you."

Carlen looked up apprehensively into his face; never had she seen there so stern a look.

"I must help mütter with the supper," she said, hesitating.

John laughed scornfully. "You were helping with the supper, I suppose, sitting out with yon tramp!" And he pointed to the stoop.

Carlen had, with all her sunny cheerfulness, a vein of her father's temper. Her face hardened, and her blue eyes grew darker.

"Why do you call Wilhelm a tramp," she said coldly.

"What is he then, if he is not a tramp?" retorted John.

"He is no tramp," she replied, still more doggedly.

"What do you know about him?" said John.

Carlen made no reply. Her silence irritated John more than any words could have done; and losing self-control, losing sight of prudence, he poured out on her a torrent of angry accusation and scornful reproach.

She stood still, her eyes fixed on the ground. Even in his hot wrath, John noticed this unwonted downcast look, and taunted her with it.

"You have even caught his miserable hangdog trick of not looking anybody in the face," he cried. "Look up now! look me in the eye, and say what you mean by all this."

Thus roughly bidden, Carlen raised her blue eyes and confronted her brother with a look hardly less angry than his own.

"It is you who have to say to me what all this means that you have been saying," she cried. "I think you are out of your senses. I do not know what has happened to you." And she turned to walk back to the house.

John seized her shoulders in his brawny hands, and whirled her round till she faced him again.

"Tell me the truth!" he said fiercely; "do you love this Wilhelm?"

Carlen opened her lips to reply. At that second a step was heard, and looking up they saw Wilhelm himself coming toward them, walking at his usual slow pace, his head sunk on his breast, his eyes on the ground. Great waves of blushes ran in tumultuous flood up Carlen's neck, cheeks, forehead. John took his hands from her shoulders, and stepped back with a look of disgust and a smothered ejaculation. Wilhelm, hearing the sound, looked up, regarded them with a cold, unchanged eye, and turned in another direction.

The color deepened on Carlen's face. In a hard and bitter tone she said, pointing with a swift gesture to Wilhelm's retreating form: "You can see for yourself that there is nothing between us. I do not know what craze has got into your head." And she walked away, this time unchecked by her brother. He needed no further replies in words. Tokens stronger than any speech had answered him. Muttering angrily to himself, he went on down to the pasture after the cows. It was a beautiful field, more like New England than Pennsylvania; a brook ran zigzagging through it, and here and there in the land were sharp lifts where rocks cropped out, making miniature cliffs overhanging some portions of the brook's-course. Gray lichens and green mosses grew on these rocks, and belts of wild flag and sedges surrounded their base. The cows, in a warm day, used to stand knee-deep there, in shade of the rocks.

It was a favorite place of Wilhelm's. He sometimes lay on the top of one of these rocks the greater part of the night, looking down into the gliding water or up into the sky. Carlen from her window had more than once seen him thus, and passionately longed to go down and comfort his lonely sorrow.

It was indeed true, as she had said to her brother, that there was "nothing between" her and Wilhelm. Never a word had passed; never a look or tone to betray that he knew whether she were fair or not, - whether she lived or not. She came and went in his presence, as did all others, with no more apparent relation to the currents of his strange veiled existence than if they or he belonged to a phantom world. But it was also true that never since the first day of his mysterious coming had Wilhelm been long absent from Carlen's thoughts; and she did indeed find him - as her father's keen eyes, sharpened by greed, had observed - good to look upon. That most insidious of love's allies, pity, had stormed the fortress of Carlen's heart, and carried it by a single charge. What could a girl give, do, or be, that would be too much for one so stricken, so lonely as was Wilhelm! The melancholy beauty of his face, his lithe figure, his great strength, all combined to heighten this impression, and to fan the flames of the passion in Carlen's virgin soul. It was indeed, as John had sorrowfully said to himself, "too late" to speak to Carlen.

As John stood now at the pasture bars, waiting for the herd of cows, slow winding up the slope from the brook, he saw Wilhelm on the rocks below. He had thrown himself down on his back, and lay there with his arms crossed on his breast. Presently he clasped both hands over his eyes as if to shut out a sight that he could no longer bear. Something akin to pity stirred even in John's angry heart as he watched him.

"What can it be," he said, "that makes him hate even the sky? It may be it is a sweetheart he has lost, and he is one of that strange kind of men who can love but once; and it is loving the dead that makes him so like one dead himself. Poor Carlen! I think myself he never so much as sees her."

A strange reverie, surely, for the brother who had so few short moments ago been angrily reproaching his sister for the disgrace and shame of caring for this tramp. But the pity was short-lived in John's bosom. His inborn distrust and antagonism to the man were too strong for any gentler sentiment toward him to live long by their side. And when the family gathered at the supper-table he fixed upon Wilhelm so suspicious and hostile a gaze that even Wilhelm's absent mind perceived it, and he in turn looked inquiringly at John, a sudden bewilderment apparent in his manner. It disappeared, however, almost immediately, dying away in his usual melancholy absorption. It had produced scarce a ripple on the monotonous surface of his habitual gloom. But Carlen had perceived all, both the look on John's face and the bewilderment on Wilhelm's; and it roused in her a resentment so fierce toward John, she could not forbear showing it. "How cruel!" she thought. "As if the poor fellow had not all he could bear already without being treated unkindly by us!" And she redoubled her efforts to win Wilhelm's attention and divert his thoughts, all in vain; kindness and unkindness glanced off alike, powerless, from the veil in which he was wrapped.

John sat by with roused attention and sharpened perception, noting all. Had it been all along like this? Where had his eyes been for the past month? Had he too been under a spell? It looked like it. He groaned in spirit as he sat silently playing with his food, not eating; and when his father said, "Why haf you not appetite, Johan?" he rose abruptly, pushed back his chair, and leaving the table without a word went out and down again into the pasture, where the dewy grass and the quivering stars in the brook shimmered in the pale light of a young moon. To John, also, the mossy rocks in this pasture were a favorite spot for rest and meditation. Since the days when he and Carlen had fished from their edges, with bent pins and yarn, for minnows, he had loved the place: they had spent happy hours enough there to count up into days; and not the least among the innumerable annoyances and irritations of which he had been anxious in regard to Wilhelm was the fact that he too had perceived the charm of the field, and chosen it for his own melancholy retreat.

As he seated himself on one of the rocks, he saw a figure gliding swiftly down the hill.

It was Carlen.

As she drew near he looked at her without speaking, but the loving girl was not repelled. Springing lightly to the rock, she threw her arms around his neck, and kissing him said: "I saw you coming down here, John, and I ran after you. Do not be angry with me, brother; it breaks my heart."

A sudden revulsion of shame for his unjust suspicion filled John with tenderness.

"Mein Schwester," he said fondly, - they had always the habit of using the German tongue for fond epithets, - "mein Schwester klein, I love you so much I cannot help being wretched when I see you in danger, but I am not angry."

Nestling herself close by his side, Carlen looked over into the water.

"This is the very rock I fell off of that day, do you

remember?" she said; "and how wet you got fishing me out! And oh, what an awful beating father gave you! and I always thought it was wicked, for if you had not pulled me out I should have drowned."

"It was for letting you fall in he beat me," laughed John; and they both grew tender and merry, recalling the babyhood times.

"How long, long ago!" cried Carlen.

"It seems only a day," said John.

"I think time goes faster for a man than for a woman," sighed Carlen. "It is a shorter day in the fields than in the house."

"Are you not content, my sister?" said John.

Carlen was silent.

"You have always seemed so," he said reproachfully.

"It is always the same, John," she murmured. "Each day like every other day. I would like it to be some days different."

John sighed. He knew of what this new unrest was born. He longed to begin to speak of Wilhelm, and yet he knew not how. Now that, after longer reflection, he had become sure in his own mind that Wilhelm cared nothing for his sister, he felt an instinctive shrinking from recognizing to himself, or letting it be recognized between them, that she unwooed had learned to love. His heart ached with dread of the suffering which might be in store for her.

Carlen herself cut the gordian knot.

"Brother," she whispered, "why do you think Wilhelm is not good?"

"I said not that, Carlen," he replied evasively. "I only say we know nothing; and it is dangerous to trust where one knows nothing."

"It would not be trust if we knew," answered the loyal girl. "I believe he is good; but, John, John, what misery in his eyes! Saw you ever anything like it?"

"No," he replied; "never. Has he never told you anything about himself, Carlen?"

"Once," she answered, "I took courage to ask him if he had relatives in Germany; and he said no; and I exclaimed then, 'What, all dead!' 'All dead,' he answered, in such a voice I hardly dared speak again, but I did. I said: 'Well, one might have the terrible sorrow to lose all one's relatives. It needs only that three should die, my father and mother and my brother, - only three, and two are already old, - and I should have no relatives myself; but if one is left without relatives, there are always friends, thank God!' And he looked at me, - he never looks at one, you know; but he looked at me then as if I had done a sin to speak the word, and he said, 'I have no friends. They are all dead too,' and then went away! Oh, brother, why cannot we win him out of this grief? We can be good friends to him; can you not find out for me what it is?"

It was a cruel weapon to use, but on the instant John made up his mind to use it. It might spare Carlen grief, in the end.

"I have thought," he said, "that it might be for a dead sweetheart he mourned thus. There are men, you know, who love that way and never smile again."

Short-sighted John, to have dreamed that he could forestall any conjecture in the girl's heart!

"I have thought of that," she answered meekly; "it would seem as if it could be nothing else. But, John, if she be really dead - " Carlen did not finish the sentence; it was not necessary.

After a silence she spoke again: "Dear John, if you could be more friendly with him I think it might be different. He is your age. Father and mother are too old, and to me he will not speak." She sighed deeply as she spoke these last words, and went on: "Of course, if it is for a dead sweetheart that he is grieving thus, it is only natural that the sight of women should be to him worse than the sight of men. But it is very seldom, John, that a man will mourn his whole life for a sweetheart; is it not, John? Why, men marry again, almost always, even when it is a wife that they have lost; and a sweetheart is not so much as a wife."

"I have heard," said the pitiless John, "that a man is quicker healed of grief for a wife than for one he had thought to wed, but lost."

"You are a man," said Carlen. "You can tell if that would be true."

"No, I cannot," he answered, "for I have loved no woman but you, my sister; and on my word I think I will be in no haste to, either. It brings misery, it seems to me."

If Carlen had spoken her thought at these words, she would have said, "Yes, it brings misery; but even so it is better than joy." But Carlen was ashamed; afraid also. She had passed now into a new life, whither her brother, she perceived, could not follow. She could barely reach his hand across the boundary line which parted them.

"I hope you will love some one, John," she said. "You would be happy with a wife. You are old enough to have a home of your own."

"Only a year older than you, my sister," he rejoined.

"I too am old enough to have a home of my own," she said, with a gentle dignity of tone, which more impressed John with a sense of the change in Carlen than all else which had been said.

It was time to return to the house. As he had done when he was ten, and she nine, John stood at the bottom of the steepest rock, with upstretched arms, by the help of which Carlen leaped lightly down.

"We are not children any more," she said, with a little laugh.

"More's the pity!" said John, half lightly, half sadly, as they went on hand in hand.

When they reached the bars, Carlen paused. Withdrawing her hand from John's and laying it on his shoulder, she said: "Brother, will you not try to find out what is Wilhelm's grief? Can you not try to be friends with him?"

John made no answer. It was a hard thing to promise.

"For my sake, brother," said the girl. "I have spoken to no one else but you. I would die before any one else should know; even my mother."

John could not resist this. "Yes," he said; "I will try. It will be hard; but I will try my best, Carlen. I will have a talk with Wilhelm to-morrow."

And the brother and sister parted, he only the sadder, she far happier, for their talk. "To-morrow," she thought, "I will know! To-morrow! oh, to-morrow!" And she fell asleep more peacefully than had been her wont for many nights.

On the morrow it chanced that John and Wilhelm went separate ways to work and did not meet until noon. In the afternoon Wilhelm was sent on an errand to a farm some five miles away, and thus the day passed without John's having found any opportunity for the promised talk. Carlen perceived with keen disappointment this frustration of his purpose, but comforted herself, thinking, with the swift forerunning trust of youth: "To-morrow he will surely get a chance. To-morrow he will have something to tell me. To-morrow!"

When Wilhelm returned from this errand, he came singing up the road. Carlen heard the voice and looked out of the window in amazement. Never before had a note of singing been heard from Wilhelm's voice. She could not believe her ears; neither her eyes, when she saw him walking swiftly, almost running, erect, his head held straight, his eyes gazing free and confident before him.

What had happened? What could have happened? Now, for the first time, Carlen saw the full beauty of his face; it wore an exultant look as of one set free, triumphant. He leaped lightly over the bars; he stooped and fondled the dog, speaking to him in a merry tone; then he whistled, then broke again into singing a gay German song. Carlen was stupefied with wonder. Who was this new man in the body of Wilhelm? Where had disappeared the man of slow-moving figure, bent head, downcast eyes, gloom-stricken face, whom until that hour she had known? Carlen clasped her hands in an agony of bewilderment.

"If he has found his sweetheart, I shall die," she thought. "How could it be? A letter, perhaps? A message?" She dreaded to see him. She lingered in her room till it was past the supper hour, dreading what she knew not, yet knew. When she went down the four were seated at supper. As she opened the door roars of laughter greeted her, and the first sight she saw was Wilhelm's face, full of vivacity, excitement. He was telling a jesting story, at which even her mother was heartily laughing. Her father had laughed till the tears were rolling down his cheeks. John was holding his sides. Wilhelm was a mimic, it appeared; he was imitating the ridiculous speech, gait, gestures, of a man he had seen in the village that afternoon.

"I sent you to village sooner as dis, if I haf known vat you are like ven you come back," said Farmer Weitbreck, wiping his eyes.

And John echoed his father. "Upon my word, Wilhelm, you are a good actor. Why have you kept your light under a bushel so long?" And John looked at him with a new interest and liking. If this were the true Wilhelm, he might welcome him indeed as a brother.

Carlen alone looked grave, anxious, unhappy. She could not laugh. Tale after tale, jest after jest, fell from Wilhelm's lips. Such a story-teller never before sat at the Weitbreck board. The old kitchen never echoed with such laughter.

Finally John exclaimed: "Man alive, where have you kept yourself all this time? Have you been ill till now, that you hid your tongue? What has cured you in a day?"

Wilhelm laughed a laugh so ringing, it made him seem like a boy.

"Yes, I have been ill till to-day," he said; "and now I am well." And he rattled on again, with his merry talk.

Carlen grew cold with fear; surely this meant but one thing. Nothing else, nothing less, could have thus in an hour rolled away the burden of his sadness.

Later in the evening she said timidly, "Did you hear any news in the village this afternoon, Wilhelm?"

"No; no news," he said. "I had heard no news."

As he said this a strange look flitted swiftly across his face, and was gone before any eye but a loving woman's had noted it. It did not escape Carlen's, and she fell into a reverie of wondering what possible double meaning could have underlain his words.

"Did you know Mr. Dietman in Germany?" she asked. This was the name of the farmer to whose house he had been sent on an errand. They were new-comers into the town, since spring.

"No!" replied Wilhelm, with another strange, sharp glance at Carlen. "I saw him not before."

"Have they children?" she continued. "Are they old?"

"No; young," he answered. "They haf one child, little baby."

Carlen could not contrive any other questions to ask. "It must have been a letter," she thought; and her face grew sadder.

It was a late bedtime when the family parted for the night. The astonishing change in Wilhelm's manner was now even more apparent than it had yet been. Instead of slipping off, as was his usual habit, without exchanging a good-night with any one, he insisted on shaking hands with each, still talking and laughing with gay and affectionate words, and repeating, over and again, "Good-night, good-night." Farmer Weitbreck was carried out of himself with pleasure at all this, and holding Wilhelm's hand fast in his, shaking it heartily, and clapping him on the shoulder, he exclaimed in fatherly familiarity: "Dis is goot, mein son! dis is goot. Now are you von of us." And he glanced meaningly at John, who smiled back in secret intelligence. As he did so there went like a flash through his mind the question, "Can Carlen have spoken with him to-day? Can that be it?" But a look at Carlen's pale, perplexed face quickly dissipated this idea. "She looks frightened," thought John. "I do not much wonder. I will get a word with her." But Carlen had gone before he missed her. Running swiftly upstairs, she locked the door of her room, and threw herself on her knees at her open window. Presently she saw Wilhelm going down to the brook. She watched his every motion. First, he walked slowly up and down the entire length of the field, following the brook's course closely, stopping often and bending over, picking flowers. A curious little white flower called "Ladies'-Tress" grew there in great abundance, and he often brought bunches of it to her.

"Perhaps it is not for me this time," thought Carlen, and the tears came into her eyes. After a time Wilhelm ceased gathering the flowers, and seated himself on his favorite rock, - the same one where John and Carlen had sat the night before. "Will he stay there all night?" thought the unhappy girl, as she watched him. "He is so full of joy he does not want to sleep. What will become of me! what will become of me!"

At last Wilhelm arose and came toward the house, bringing the bunch of flowers in his hand. At the pasture bars he paused, and looked back over the scene. It was a beautiful picture, the moon making it light as day; even from Carlen's window could be seen the sparkle of the brook.

As he turned to go to the barn his head sank on his breast, his steps lagged. He wore again the expression of gloomy thought. A new fear arose in Carlen's breast. Was he mad? Had the wild hilarity of his speech and demeanor in the evening been merely a new phase of disorder in an unsettled brain? Even in this was a strange, sad comfort to Carlen. She would rather have him mad, with alternations of insane joy and gloom, than know that he belonged to another. Long after he had disappeared in the doorway at the foot of the stairs

Helen Hunt Jackson

which led to his sleeping-place in the barn-loft, she remained kneeling at the window, watching to see if he came out again. Then she crept into bed, and lay tossing, wakeful, and anxious till near dawn. She had but just fallen asleep when she was aroused by cries. It was John's voice. He was calling loudly at the window of their mother's bedroom beneath her own.

"Father! father! Get up, quick! Come out to the barn!"

Then followed confused words she could not understand. Leaning from her window she called: "What is it, John? What has happened?" But he was already too far on his way back to the barn to hear her.

A terrible presentiment shot into her mind of some ill to Wilhelm. Vainly she wrestled with it. Why need she think everything that happened must be connected with him? It was not yet light; she could not have slept many minutes. With trembling hands she dressed, and running swiftly down the stairs was at the door just as her father appeared there.

"What is it? What is it, father?" she cried. "What has happened?"

"Go back!" he said in an unsteady voice. "It is nothing. Go back to bed. It is not for vimmins!"

Then Carlen was sure it was some ill to Wilhelm, and with a loud cry she darted to the barn, and flew up the stairway leading to his room.

John, hearing her steps, confronted her at the head of the stairs.

"Good God, Carlen!" he cried, "go back! You must not come here. Where is father?"

"I will come in!" she answered wildly, trying to force her way past him. "I will come in. You shall not keep me out. What has happened to him? Let me by!" And she wrestled in her brother's strong arms with strength almost equal to his.

"Carlen! You shall not come in! You shall not see!" he cried.

"Shall not see!" she shrieked. "Is he dead?"

"Yes, my sister, he is dead," answered John, solemnly. In the next instant he held Carlen's unconscious form in his arms; and when Farmer Weitbreck, half dazed, reached the foot of the stairs, the first sight which met his eyes was his daughter, held in her brother's arms, apparently lifeless, her head hanging over his shoulder.

"Haf she seen him?" he whispered.

"No!" said John. "I only told her he was dead, to keep her from going in, and she fainted dead away."

"Ach!" groaned the old man, "dis is hard on her."

"Yes," sighed the brother; "it is a cruel shame."

Swiftly they carried her to the house, and laid her on her mother's bed, then returned to their dreadful task in Wilhelm's chamber.

Hung by a stout leathern strap from the roof-tree beam, there swung the dead body of Wilhelm Rütter, cold, stiff. He had been dead for hours; he must have done the deed soon after bidding them good-night.

"He vas mad, Johan; it must be he vas mad ven he laugh like dat last night. Dat vas de beginning, Johan," said the old man, shaking from head to foot with horror, as he helped his son lift down the body.

"Yes!" answered John; "that must be it. I expect he has been mad all along. I do not believe last night was the beginning. It was not like any sane man to be so gloomy as he was, and never speak to a living soul. But I never once thought of his being crazy. Look, father!" he continued, his voice breaking into a sob, "he has left these flowers here for Carlen! That does not look as if he was crazy! What can it all mean?"

On the top of a small chest lay the bunch of white Ladies'-Tress, with a paper beneath it on which was written, "For Carlen Weitbreck, - these, and the carvings in the box, all in memory of Wilhelm."

"He meant to do it, den," said the old man.

"Yes," said John.

"Maybe Carlen vould not haf him, you tink?"

"No," said John, hastily; "that is not possible."

"I tought she luf him, an' he vould stay an' be her mann," sighed the disappointed father. "Now all dat is no more."

"It will kill her," cried John.

"No!" said the father. "Vimmins does not die so as dat. She feel pad maybe von year, maybe two. Dat is all. He vas great for vork. Dat Alf vas not goot as he."

The body was laid once more on the narrow pallet where it had slept for its last few weeks on earth, and the two men stood by its side, discussing what should next be done, how the necessary steps could be taken with least possible publicity, when suddenly they heard the sound of horses' feet and wheels, and looking out they saw Hans Dietman and his wife driving rapidly into the yard.

"Mein Gott! Vat bring dem here dis time in day," exclaimed Farmer Weitbreck. "If dey ask for Wilhelm dey must all know!"

"Yes," replied John; "that makes no difference. Everybody will have to know." And he ran swiftly down to meet the strangely arrived neighbors.

His first glance at their faces showed him that they had come on no common errand. They were pale and full of excitement, and Hans's first word was: "Vere is dot man you sent to mine place yesterday?"

"Wilhelm?" stammered Farmer Weitbreck.

"Wilhelm!" repeated Hans, scornfully. "His name is not 'Wilhelm.' His name is Carl, - Carl Lepmann; and he is murderer. He killed von man - shepherd, in our town - last spring; and dey never get trail of him. So soon he came in our kitchen yesterday my vife she knew him; she wait till I get home. Ve came ven it vas yet dark to let you know vot man vas in your house."

Farmer Weitbreck and his son exchanged glances; each was too shocked to speak. Mr. and Mrs. Dietman looked from one to the other in bewilderment. "Maype you tink ve speak not truth," Hans continued. "Just let him come here, to our face, and you will see."

"No!" said John, in a low, awe-stricken voice, "we do not think you are not speaking truth." He paused; glanced again at his father. "We'd better take them up!" he said.

The old man nodded silently. Even his hard and phlegmatic nature was shaken to the depths.

John led the way up the stairs, saying briefly, "Come." The Dietmans followed in bewilderment.

"There he is," said John, pointing to the tall figure, rigid, under the close-drawn white folds; "we found him here only an hour ago, hung from the beam."

A horror-stricken silence fell on the group.

Hans spoke first. "He know dat we know; so he kill himself to save dat de hangman have trouble."

John resented the flippant tone. He understood now the whole mystery of Wilhelm's life in this house.

"He has never known a happy minute since he was here," he said. "He never smiled; nor spoke, if he could help it. Only last night, after he came back from your place, he laughed and sang, and was merry, and looked like another man; and he bade us all good-night over and over, and shook hands with every one. He had made up his mind, you see, that the end had come, and it was nothing but a relief to him. He was glad to die. He had not courage before. But now he knew he would be arrested he had courage to kill himself. Poor fellow, I pity him!" And John smoothed out the white folds over the clasped hands on the quiet-stricken breast, resting at last. "He has been worse punished than if he had been hung in the beginning," he said, and turned from the bed, facing the Dietmans as if he constituted himself the dead man's protector.

"I think no one but ourselves need know," he continued, thinking in his heart of Carlen. "It is enough that he is dead. There is no good to be gained for any one, that I see, by telling what he had done."

"No," said Mrs. Dietman, tearfully; but her husband exclaimed, in a vindictive tone:

"I see not why it is to be covered in secret. He is murderer. It is to be sent vord to Mayence he vas found."

"Yes, they ought to know there," said John, slowly; "but there is no need for it to be known here. He has injured no one here."

"No," exclaimed Farmer Weitbreck. "He haf harm nobody here; he vas goot. I haf ask him to stay and haf home in my house."

It was a strange story. Early in the spring, it seemed, about six weeks before Hans Dietman and his wife Gretchen were married, a shepherd on the farm adjoining Gretchen's father's had been murdered by a fellow-laborer on the same farm. They had had high words about a dog, and had come to blows, but were parted by some of the other hands, and had separated and gone their ways to their work with their respective flocks.

This was in the morning. At night neither they nor their flocks returned; and, search being made, the dead body of the younger shepherd was found lying at the foot of a precipice, mutilated and wounded, far more than it would have been by any accidental fall. The other shepherd, Carl Lepmann, had disappeared, and was never again seen by any one who knew him, until this previous day, when he had entered the Dietmans' door bearing his message from the Weitbreck farm. At the first sight of his face, Gretchen Dietman had recognized him, thrown up her arms involuntarily, and cried out in German: "My God! the man that killed the shepherd!" Carl had halted on the threshold at hearing these words, and his countenance had changed; but it was only for a second. He regained his composure instantly, entered as if he had heard nothing, delivered his message, and afterward remained for some time on the farm chatting with the laborers, and seeming in excellent spirits.

"And so vas he ven he come home," said Farmer Weitbreck; "he make dat ve all laugh and laugh, like notings ever vas before, never before he open his mouth to speak; he vas like at funeral all times, night and day. But now he seem full of joy. It is de most strange ting as I haf seen in my life."

"I do not think so, father," said John. "I do not wonder he was glad to be rid of his burden."

It proved of no use to try to induce Hans Dietman to keep poor Carl's secret. He saw no reason why a murderer should be sheltered from disgrace. To have his name held up for the deserved execration seemed to Hans the only punishment left for one who had thus evaded the hangman; and he proceeded to inflict this punishment to the extent of his ability.

Finding that the tale could not be kept secret, John nerved himself to tell it to Carlen. She heard it in silence from beginning to end, asked a few searching questions, and then to John's unutterable astonishment said: "Wilhelm never killed that man. You have none of you stopped to see if there was proof."

"But why did he fly, Liebchen?" asked John.

"Because he knew he would be accused of the murder," she replied. "They might have been fighting at the edge of the precipice and the shepherd fell over, or the shepherd might have been killed by some one else, and Wilhelm have found the body. He never killed him, John, never."

There was something in Carlen's confident belief which communicated itself to John's mind, and, coupled with the fact that there was certainly only circumstantial evidence against Wilhelm, slowly brought him to sharing her belief and tender sorrow. But they were alone in this belief and alone in their sorrow. The verdict of the community was unhesitatingly, unqualifiedly, against Wilhelm.

"Would a man hang himself if he knew he were innocent?" said everybody.

"All the more if he knew he could never prove himself innocent," said John and Carlen. But no one else thought so. And how could the truth ever be known in this world?

Wilhelm was buried in a corner of the meadow field he had so loved. Before two years had passed, wild blackberry vines had covered the grave with a thick mat of tangled leaves, green in summer, blood-red in the autumn. And before three more had passed there was no one in the place who knew the secret of the grave. Farmer Weitbreck and his wife were both dead, and the estate had passed into the hands of strangers who had heard the story of Wilhelm, and knew that his body was buried somewhere on the farm; but in which field they neither asked nor cared, and there was no mourner to tell the story. John Weitbreck had realized his dream of going West, a free man at last, and by no means a poor one; he looked out over scores of broad fields of his own, one of the most fertile of the Oregon valleys.

Alf was with him, and Carlen; and Carlen was Alf's wife, - placid, contented wife, and fond and happy mother, - so small ripples did there remain from the tempestuous waves beneath which Carl Lepmann's life had gone down. Some deftly carved boxes and figures of chamois and their hunters stood on Carlen's best-room mantel, much admired by her neighbors, and longed for by her toddling girl, - these, and a bunch of dried and crumbling blossoms of the Ladies' Tress, were all that had survived the storm. The dried flowers were in the largest of the boxes. They lay there side by side with a bit of carved abalone shell Alf had got from a Nez Perce Indian, and some curious seaweeds he had picked up at the mouth of the Columbia River. Carlen's one gilt brooch was kept in the same box, and when she took it out of a Sunday, the sight of the withered flowers always reminded her of Wilhelm. She could not have told why she kept them; it certainly was not because they woke in her breast any thoughts which Alf might not have read without being disquieted. She sometimes sighed, as she saw them, "Poor Wilhelm!" That was all.

But there came one day a letter to John that awoke even in Carlen's motherly and contented heart strange echoes from that past which she had thought forever left behind. It was a letter from Hans Dietman, who still lived on the Pennsylvania farm, and who had been recently joined there by a younger brother from Germany.

This brother had brought news which, too late, vindicated the memory of Wilhelm. Carlen had been right. He was no murderer.

It was with struggling emotions that Carlen heard the tale; pride, joy, passionate regret, old affection, revived. John was half afraid to go on, as he saw her face flushing, her eyes filling with tears, kindling and shining with a light he had not seen in them since her youth.

"Go on! go on!" she cried. "Why do you stop? Did I not tell you so? And you never half believed me! Now you see I was right! I told you Wilhelm never harmed a human being!"

It was indeed a heartrending story, to come so late, so bootless now, to the poor boy who had slept all these years in the nameless grave, even its place forgotten.

It seemed that a man sentenced in Mayence to be

executed for murder had confessed, the day before his execution, that it was he who had killed the shepherd of whose death Carl Lepmann had so long been held guilty. They had quarrelled about a girl, a faithless creature, forsworn to both of them, and worth no man's love or desire; but jealous anger got the better of their sense, and they grappled in fight, each determined to kill the other.

The shepherd had the worst of it; and just as he fell, mortally hurt, Carl Lepmann had come up, - had come up in time to see the murderer leap on his horse to ride away.

In a voice, which the man said had haunted him ever since, Carl had cried out: "My God! You ride away and leave him dead! and it will be I who have killed him, for this morning we fought so they had to tear us apart!"

Smitten with remorse, the man had with Carl's help lifted the body and thrown it over the precipice, at the foot of which it was afterward found. He then endeavored to persuade the lad that it would never be discovered, and he might safely return to his employer's farm. But Carl's terror was too great, and he had finally been so wrought upon by his entreaties that he had taken him two days' journey, by lonely ways, the two riding sometimes in turn, sometimes together, - two days' and two nights' journey, - till they reached the sea, where Carl had taken ship for America.

"He was a good lad, a tender-hearted lad," said the murderer. "He might have accused me in many a village, and stood as good chance to be believed as I, if he had told where the shepherd's body was thrown; but he could be frightened as easily as a woman, and all he thought of was to fly where he would never be heard of more. And it was the thought of him, from that day till now, has given me more misery than the thought of the dead man!"

Carlen was crying bitterly; the letter was just ended, when Alf came into the room asking bewilderedly what it was all about.

The name Wilhelm meant nothing to him. It was the summer before Wilhelm came that he had begun this Oregon farm, which he, from the first, had fondly dedicated to Carlen in his thoughts; and when he went back to Pennsylvania after her, he found her the same as when he went away, only comelier and sweeter. It would not be easy to give Alf an uncomfortable thought about his Carlen. But he did not like to see her cry.

Neither, when he had heard the whole story, did he see why her tears need have flowed so freely. It was sad, no doubt, and a bitter shame too, for one man to suffer and go to his grave that way for the sin of another. But it was long past and gone; no use in crying over it now.

"What a tender-hearted, foolish wife it is!" he said in gruff fondness, laying his hand on Carlen's shoulder, "crying over a man dead and buried these seven years, and none of our kith or kin, either. Poor fellow! It was a shame!"

But Carlen said nothing.

Little Bel's Supplement.

"Indeed, then, my mother, I'll not take the school at Wissan Bridge without they promise me a supplement. It's the worst school i' a' Prince Edward Island."

"I doubt but ye're young to tackle wi' them boys, Bel," replied the mother, gazing into her daughter's face with an intent expression in which it would have been hard to say which predominated, - anxiety or fond pride. "I'd sooner see ye take any other school between this an' Charlottetown, an' no supplement."

"I'm not afraid, my mother, but I'll manage 'em well enough; but I'll not undertake it for the same money as a decent school is taught. They'll promise me five pounds' supplement at the end o' the year, or I'll not set foot i' the place."

"Maybe they'll not be for givin' ye the school at all when they see what's yer youth," replied the mother, in a half-antagonistic tone. There was between this mother and daughter a continual undercurrent of possible antagonism, overlain and usually smothered out of sight by passionate attachment on both sides.

Little Bel tossed her head. "Age is not everything that goes to the makkin o' a teacher," she retorted. "There's Grizzy McLeod; she's teachin' at the Cove these eight years, an' I'd shame her myself any day she likes wi' spellin' an' the lines; an' if there's ever a boy in a school o' mine that'll gie me a floutin' answer such's I've heard her take by the dozen, I'll warrant ye he'll get a birchin'; an' the trustees think there's no teacher like Grizzy. I'm not afraid."

"Grizzy never had any great schoolin' herself," replied her mother, piously. "There's no girl in all the farms that's had what ye've had, Bel."

"It isn't the schoolin', mother," retorted little Bel. "The schoolin' 's got nothin' to do with it. I'd teach a school better than Grizzy McLeod if I'd never had a day's schoolin'."

"An' now if that's not the talk of a silly," retorted the quickly angered parent. "Will ye be tellin' me perhaps, then, that them that can't read theirselves is to be set to teach letters?"

Little Bel was too loyal at heart to her illiterate mother to wound her further by reiterating her point. Throwing her arms around her neck, and kissing her warmly, she exclaimed: "Eh, my mother, it's not a silly that ye could ever have for a child, wi' that clear head, and the wise things always said to us from the time we're in our cradles. Ye've never a child that's so clever as ye are yerself. I didn't mean just what I said, ye must know, surely; only that the schoolin' part is the smallest part o' the keepin' a school."

"An' I'll never give in to such nonsense as that, either," said the mother, only half mollified. "Ye can ask yer father, if ye like, if it stands not to reason that the more a teacher knows, the more he can teach. He'll take the conceit out o' ye better than I can." And good Isabella McDonald turned angrily away, and drummed on the window-pane with her knitting-needles to relieve her nervous discomfort at this slight passage at arms with her best-beloved daughter.

Little Bel's face flushed, and with compressed lips she turned silently to the little oaken-framed looking-glass that hung so high on the wall she could but just see her chin in it. As she slowly tied her pink bonnet strings she grew happier. In truth, she would have been a maiden hard to console if the face that looked back at her from the quaint oak leaf and acorn wreath had not comforted her inmost soul, and made her again at peace with herself. And as the mother looked on she too was comforted; and in five minutes more, when Little Bel was ready to say good-by, they flung their arms around each other, and embraced and kissed, and the daughter said, "Good-by t' ye now, mother. Wish me well, an' ye'll see that I get it, - supplement an' all," she added slyly. And the mother said, "Good luck t' ye, child; an' it's luck to them that gets ye." That was the way quarrels always ended between Isabella McDonald and her oldest daughter.

The oldest daughter, and yet only just turned of twenty; and there were eight children younger than she, and one older. This is the way among the Scotch farming-folk in Prince Edward Island. Children come tumbling into the world like rabbits in a pen, and have to scramble for a living almost as soon and as hard as the rabbits. It is a narrow life they lead, and full of hardships and deprivations, but it has its compensations. Sturdy virtues in sturdy bodies come of it, - the sort of virtue made by the straitest Calvinism, and the sort of body made out of oatmeal and milk. One might do much worse than inherit both.

It seemed but a few years ago that John McDonald had wooed and won Isabella McIntosh, - wooed her with difficulty in the bosom of her family of six brothers and five sisters, and won her triumphantly in spite of the open and contemptuous opposition of one of the five sisters. For John himself was one of seven in his father's home, and whoever married John must go there to live, to be only a daughter in a mother-in-law's house, and take a daughter's share of the brunt of everything. "And nothing to be got except a living, and it was a poor living the McDonald farm gave beside the McIntosh," the McIntosh sisters said. And, moreover: "The saint did not live that could get on with John McDonald's mother. That was what had made him the silent fellow he was, always being told by his mother to hold his tongue and have done speaking; and a fine pepper-pot there'd be when Isabella's hasty tongue and temper were flung into that batch!"

There was no gainsaying all this. Nevertheless, Isabella married John, went home with him into his father's house, put her shoulder against her spoke in the family wheel, and did her best. And when, ten years later, as reward of her affectionate trust and patience, she found herself sole mistress of the McDonald farm, she did not feel herself ill paid. The old father and mother were dead, two sisters had died and two had married, and the two sons had gone to the States to seek better fortunes than were to be made on Prince Edward Island. John, as eldest son, had, according to the custom of the island, inherited the farm; and Mrs. Isabella, confronting her three still unmarried sisters, was able at last triumphantly to refute their still resentfully remembered objections to her choice of a husband.

"An' did ye suppose I did not all the time know that it was to this it was sure to come, soon or late?" she said, with justifiable complacency. "It's a good thing to have a house o' one's own an' an estate. An' the linen that's in the house! I've no need to turn a hand to the flax-wheel for ten years if I've no mind. An' ye can all bide your times, an' see what John'll make o' the farm, now he's got where he can have things his own way. His father was always set against anything that was new, an' the place is run down shameful; but John'll bring it up, an' I'm not an old woman yet."

This last was the unkindest phrase Mrs. John McDonald permitted herself to use. There was a rebound in it which told on the McIntosh sisters; for they, many years older than she, were already living on tolerance in their father's house, where their oldest brother and his wife ruled things with an iron hand. All hopes of a husband and a home of their own had quite died out of their spinster bosoms, and they would not have been human had they not secretly and grievously envied the comely, blooming Isabella her husband, children, and home.

But, with all this, it was no play-day life that Mrs. Isabella had led. At the very best, and with the best of farms, Prince Edward Island farming is no high-road to fortune; only a living, and that of the plainest, is to be made; and when children come at the rate of ten in twenty-two years, it is but a small showing that the farmer's bank account makes at the end of that time. There is no margin for fineries, luxuries, small ambitions of any kind. Isabella had her temptations in these directions, but John was firm as a rock in withstanding them. If he had not been, there would never have been this story to tell of his Little Bel's school-teaching, for there would never have been money enough in the bank to have given her two years' schooling in Charlottetown, the best the little city afforded, - "and she boardin' all the time like a lady," said the severe McIntosh aunts, who disapproved of all such wide-flying ambitions, which made women discontented with and unfitted for farming life.

"And why should Isabella be setting her daughters up for teachers?" they said. "It's no great schoolin' she had herself, and if her girls do as well as she's done, they'll be lucky," - a speech which made John McDonald laugh out when it was reported to him. He could afford to laugh now.

"I mind there was a day when they thought different o' me from that," he said. "I'm obliged to them for nothin'; but I'd like the little one to have a better chance than the marryin' o' a man like me, an' if anything'll get it for her, it'll be schoolin'."

The "boardin' like a lady," which had so offended the Misses McIntosh's sense of propriety, was not, after all, so great an extravagance as they had supposed; for it was in his own brother's house her thrifty father had put her, and had stipulated that part of the price of her board was to be paid in produce of one sort and another from the farm, at market rates; "an' so, ye see, the lass 'll be eatin' it there 'stead of here," he said to his wife when he told her of the arrangement, "an' it's a sma' difference it'll make to us i' the end o' the two years."

"An' a big difference to her a' her life," replied Isabella, warmly.

"Ay, wife," said John, "if it fa's out as ye hope; but it's main uncertain countin' on the book-knowledge. There's some it draws up an' some it draws down; it's a millstone. But the lass is bright; she's as like you as two peas in a pod. If ye'd had the chance she's had - "

Rising color in Isabella's face warned John to stop. It is a strange thing to see how often there hovers a flitting shadow of jealousy between a mother and the daughter to whom the father unconsciously manifests a chivalrous tenderness akin to that which in his youth he had given only to the sweetheart he sought for wife. Unacknowledged, perhaps, even unmanifested save in occasional swift and unreasonable petulances, it is still there, making many a heartache, which is none the less bitter that it is inexplicable to itself, and dares not so much as confess its own existence.

"It's a better thing for a woman to make her way i' the world on the book-learnin' than to be always at the wheel an' the churn an' the floors to be whitened," replied Isabella, sharply. "An' one year like another, till the year comes ye're buried. I look for Bel to marry a minister, or maybe even better."

"Ye'd a chance at a minister yersel', then, my girl," replied the wise John, "an' ye did not take it." At which memory the wife laughed, and the two loyal hearts were merry together for a moment, and young again.

Little Bel had, indeed, even before the Charlottetown schooling, had a far better chance than her mother; for in her mother's day there was no free school in the island, and in families of ten and twelve it was only a turn and turn about that the children had at school. Since the free schools had been established many a grown man and woman had sighed curiously at the better luck of the youngsters under the new regime. No excuse now for the poorest man's children not knowing how to read and write and more; and if they chose to keep on, nothing to hinder their dipping into studies of which their parents never heard so much as the names.

And this was not the only better chance which Little Bel had had. John McDonald's farm joined the lands of the manse; his house was a short mile from the manse itself; and by a bit of good fortune for Little Bel it happened that just as she was growing into girlhood there came a new minister to the manse, - a young man from Halifax, with a young bride, the daughter of an officer in the Halifax garrison, - gentlefolks, both of them, but single-hearted and full of fervor in their work for the souls of the plain farming-people given into their charge. And both Mr. Allan and Mrs. Allan had caught sight of Little Bel's face on their first Sunday in church, and Mrs. Allan had traced to her a flute-like voice she had detected in the Sunday-school singing; and before long, to Isabella's great but unspoken pride, the child had been "bidden to the manse for the minister's wife to hear her sing;" and from that day there was a new vista in Little Bel's life.

Her voice was sweet as a lark's and as pure, and her passionate love for music a gift in itself. "It would be a sin not to cultivate it," said Mrs. Allan to her husband, "even if she never sees another piano than mine, nor has any other time in her life except these few years to enjoy it; she will always have had these, and nothing can separate her from her voice."

And so it came to pass that when, at sixteen, Little Bel went to Charlottetown for her final two years of study at the High School, she played almost as well as Mrs. Allan herself, and sang far better. And in all Isabella McDonald's day-dreams of the child's future, vague or minute, there was one feature never left out. The "good husband" coming always was to be a man who could "give her a piano."

In Charlottetown Bel found no such friend as Mrs. Allan; but she had a young school-mate who had a piano, and - poor short-sighted creature that she was, Bel thought - hated the sight of it, detested to practise, and shed many a tear over her lessons. This girl's parents were thankful to see their daughter impressed by Bel's enthusiasm for music; and so well did the clever girl play her cards that before she had been six months in the place, she was installed as music-teacher to her own schoolfellow, earning thereby not only money enough to buy the few clothes she needed, but, what to her was better than money, the privilege of the use of the piano an hour a day.

So when she went home, at the end of the two years, she had lost nothing, - in fact, had made substantial progress; and her old friend and teacher, Mrs. Allan, was as proud as she was astonished when she first heard her play and sing. Still more astonished was she at the forceful character the girl had developed. She went away a gentle, loving, clinging child; her nature, like her voice, belonging to the order of birds, - bright, flitting, merry, confiding. She returned a woman, still loving, still gentle in her manner, but with a new poise in her bearing, a resoluteness, a fire, of which her first girlhood had given no suggestion. It was strange to see how similar yet unlike were the comments made on her in the manse and in the farmhouse by the two couples most interested in her welfare.

"It is wonderful, Robert," said Mrs. Allan to her husband, "how that girl has changed, and yet not changed. It is the music that has lifted her up so. What a glorious thing is a real passion for any art in a human soul! But she can never live here among these people. I must take her to Halifax."

"No," said Mr. Allan; "her work will be here. She belongs to her people in heart, all the same. She will not be discontented."

"Husband, I'm doubtin' if we've done the right thing by the child, after a'," said the mother, tearfully, to the father, at the end of the first evening after Bel's return. "She's got the ways o' the city on her, an' she carries herself as if she'd be teachin' the minister his own self. I doubt but she'll feel herself strange i' the house."

"Never you fash yourself," replied John. "The girl's got her head, that's a'; but her heart's i' the right place. Ye'll see she'll put her strength to whatever there's to be done. She'll be a master hand at teachin', I'll wager!"

"You always did think she was perfection," replied the mother, in a crisp but not ill-natured tone, "an' I'm not gainsayin' that she's not as near it as is often seen; but I'm main uneasy to see h er carryin' herself so positive."

If John thought in his heart that Bel had come through direct heredity on the maternal side by this "carryin' herself positive," he knew better than to say so, and his only reply was a good-natured laugh, with: "You'll see!

I'm not afraid. She's a good child, an' always was."

Bel passed her examination triumphantly, and got the Wissan Bridge school; but she got only a contingent promise of the five-pound supplement. It went sorely against her will to waive this point. Very keenly Mr. Allan, who was on the Examining Board, watched her face as she modestly yet firmly pressed it.

The trustees did not deny that the Wissan Bridge school was a difficult and unruly one; that to manage it well was worth more money than the ordinary school salaries. The question was whether this very young lady could manage it at all; and if she failed, as the last incumbent had, - failed egregiously, too; the school had broken up in riotous confusion before the end of the year, - the canny Scotchmen of the School Board did not wish to be pledged to pay that extra five pounds. The utmost Bel could extract from them was a promise that if at the end of the year her teaching had proved satisfactory, the five pounds should be paid. More they would not say; and after a short, sharp struggle with herself Bel accepted the terms; but she could not restrain a farewell shot at the trustees as she turned to go. "I'm as sure o' my five pounds as if ye'd promised it downright, sirs. I shall keep ye a good school at Wissan Bridge."

"We'll make it guineas, then, Miss Bel," cried Mr. Allan, enthusiastically, looking at his colleagues, who nodded their heads, and said, laughing, "Yes, guineas it is."

"And guineas it will be," retorted Little Bel, as with cheeks like peonies she left the room.

"Egad, but she's a fine spirit o' her ain, an' as bonnie a face as I've seen since I remember," cried old Mr. Dalgetty, the senior member of the Board, and the one hardest to please. "I'd not mind bein' a pupil at Wissan Bridge school the comin' term myself." And he gave an old man's privileged chuckle as he looked at his colleagues. "But she's over-young for the work, - over-young."

"She'll do it," said Mr. Allan, confidently. "Ye need have no fear. My wife's had the training of the girl since she was little. She's got the best o' stuff in her. She'll do it."

Mr. Allan's prediction was fulfilled. Bel did it. But she did it at the cost of harder work than even she had anticipated. If it had not been for her music she would never have pulled through with the boys of Wissan Bridge. By her music she tamed them. The young Marsyas himself never piped to a wilder set of creatures than the uncouth lads and young men that sat in wide-eyed, wide-mouthed astonishment listening to the first song their pretty young schoolmistress sang for them. To have singing exercises part of the regular school routine was a new thing at Wissan Bridge. It took like wild-fire; and when Little Bel, shrewd and diplomatic as a statesman, invited the two oldest and worst boys in the school to come Wednesday and Saturday afternoons to her boarding-place to practise singing with her to the accompaniment of the piano, so as to be able to help her lead the rest, her sovereignty was established. They were not conquered; they were converted, - a far surer and more lasting process. Neither of them would, from that day out, have been guilty of an act, word, or look to annoy her, any more than if they had been rival lovers suing for her hand.

As Bel's good luck would have it, - and Bel was born to good luck, there is no denying it, - one of these boys had a good tenor voice, the other a fine barytone; they had both in their rough way been singers all their lives, and were lovers of music.

"That was more than half the battle, my mother," confessed Bel, when, at the end of the first term she was at home for a few days, and was recounting her experiences. "Except for the singin' I'd never have got Archie McLeod under, nor Sandy Stairs either. I doubt they'd have been too many for me, but now they're like two more teachers to the fore. I'd leave the school-room to them for a day, an' not a lad'd dare stir in his seat without their leave. I call them my constables; an' I'm teaching them a small bit of chemistry out o' school hours, too, an' that's a hold on them. They'll see me out safe; an' I'm thinkin' I'll owe them a bit part o' the five guineas when I get it," she added reflectively.

"The minister says ye're sure of it," replied her mother. "He says ye've the best school a'ready in all his circuit. I don't know how ever ye come to't so quick, child." And Isabella McDonald smiled wistfully, spite of all her pride in her clever bairn.

"Ye see, then, what he'll say after the examination at New Year's," gleefully replied Bel, "if he thinks the school is so good now. It'll be twice as good then; an' such singin' as was never heard before in any school-house on the island, I'll warrant me. I'm to have the piano over for the day to the school-house. Archie and Sandy'll move it in a big wagon, to save me payin' for the cartin'; an' I'm to pay a half-pound for the use of it if it's not hurt, - a dear bargain, but she'd not let it go a shilling less. And, to be sure, there is the risk to be counted. An' she knew I 'd have it if it had been twice that. But I got it out of her that for that price she was to let me have all the school over twice a week, for two months before, to practise. So it's not too dear. Ye'll see what ye'll hear then."

It had been part of Little Bel's good luck that she had succeeded in obtaining board in the only family in the village which had the distinction of owning a piano; and by paying a small sum extra, she had obtained the use of this piano for an hour each day, - the best investment of Little Bel's life, as the sequel showed.

It was a bitter winter on Prince Edward Island. By New Year's time the roads were many of them wellnigh impassable with snow. Fierce winds swept to and fro, obliterating tracks by noon which had been clear in the morning; and nobody went abroad if he could help it. New Year's Day opened fiercest of all, with scurries of snow, lowering sky, and a wind that threatened to be a gale before night. But, for all that, the tying-posts behind the Wissan Bridge school-house were crowded full of steaming horses under buffalo-robes, which must stamp and paw and shiver, and endure the day as best they might, while the New Year's examination went on. Everybody had come. The fame of the singing of the Wissan Bridge school had spread far and near, and it had been whispered about that there was to be a "piece" sung which was finer than anything ever sung in the Charlottetown churches.

The school-house was decorated with evergreens, - pine and spruce. The New Year's Day having fallen on a Monday, Little Bel had had a clear working-day on the Saturday previous; and her faithful henchmen, Archie and Sandy, had been busy every evening for a week drawing the boughs on their sleds and piling them up in the yard. The teacher's desk had been removed, and in its place stood the shining red mahogany piano, - a new and wonderful sight to many eyes there.

All was ready, the room crowded full, and the Board of Trustees not yet arrived. There sat their three big arm-chairs on the raised platform, empty, - a depressing and perplexing sight to Little Bel, who, in her short blue merino gown, with a knot of pink ribbon at her throat, and a roll of white paper (her schedule of exercises) in her hand, stood on the left hand of the piano, her eyes fixed expectantly on the doors. The minutes lengthen-ed out into quarter of an hour, half an hour. Anxiously Bel consulted with her father what should be done.

"The roads are something fearfu', child," he replied; "we must make big allowance for that. They're sure to be comin', at least some one o' them. It was never known that they failed on the New Year's examination, an' it would seem a sore disrespect to begin without them here."

Before he had finished speaking there was heard a merry jingling of bells outside, dozens and dozens it seemed, and hilarious voices and laughter, and the snorting of overdriven horses, and the stamping of feet, and more voices and more laughter. Everybody looked in his neighbor's face. What sounds were these? Who ever heard a sober School Board arrive in such fashion as this? But it was the School Board, - nothing less: a good deal more, however. Little Bel's heart sank within her as she saw the foremost figure entering the room. What evil destiny had brought Sandy Bruce in the character of school visitor that day? - Sandy Bruce, retired school-teacher himself, superintendent of the hospital in Charlottetown, road-master, ship-owner, exciseman, - Sandy Bruce, whose sharp and unexpected questions had been known to floor the best of scholars and upset the plans of the best of teachers. Yes, here he was, - Sandy Bruce himself; and it was his fierce little Norwegian ponies, with their silver bells and fur collars, the admiration of all Charlottetown, that had made such a clatter and stamping outside, and were still keeping it up; for every time they stirred the bells tinkled like a peal of chimes. And, woe upon woe, behind him came, not Bel's friend and pastor, Mr. Allan, but the crusty old Dalgetty, whose doing it had been a year before, as Bel very well knew, that the five-pound supplement had been only conditionally promised.

Conflicting emotions turned Bel's face scarlet as she advanced to meet them; the most casual observer could not have failed to see that dismay predominated, and Sandy Bruce was no casual observer; nothing escaped his keen glance and keener intuition, and it was almost with a wicked twinkle in his little hazel eyes that he said, still shaking off the snow, stamping and puffing: "Eh, but ye were not lookin' for me, teacher! The minister was sent for to go to old Elspie Breadalbane, who's dyin' the morn; and I happened by as he was startin', an' he made me promise to come i' his place; an' I picked up my friend Dalgetty here a few miles back, wi' his horse flounderin' i' the drifts. Except for me ye'd ha' had no board at all here to-day; so I hope ye'll give me no bad welcome."

As he spoke he was studying her face, where the color came and went like waves; not a thought in the girl's heart he did not read. "Poor little lassie!" he was thinking to himself. "She's shaking in her shoes with fear o' me. I'll not put her out. She's a dainty blossom of a girl. What's kept her from being trodden down by these Wissan Bridge racketers, I'd like to know."

But when he seated himself on the platform, and took his first look at the rows of pupils in the centre of the room, he was near starting with amazement. The Wissan Bridge "racketers," as he had mentally called them, were not to be seen. Very well he knew many of them by sight; for his shipping business called him often to Wissan Bridge, and this was not the first time he had been inside the school-house, which had been so long the dread and terror of school boards and teachers alike. A puzzled frown gathered between Sandy Bruce's eyebrows as he gazed.

"What has happened to the youngsters, then? Have they all been converted i' this twelvemonth?" he was thinking. And the flitting perplexed thought did not escape the observation of John McDonald, who was as quick a reader of faces as Sandy himself, and had been by no means free from anxiety for his little Bel when he saw the redoubtable visage of the exciseman appear in the doorway.

"He's takin' it in quick the way the bairn's got them a' in hand," thought John. "If only she can hold hersel' cool now!"

No danger. Bel was not the one to lose a battle by appearing to quail in the outset, however clearly she might see herself outnumbered. And sympathetic and eager glances from her constables, Archie and Sandy, told her that they were all ready for the fray. These glances Sandy Bruce chanced to intercept, and they heightened his bewilderment. To Archie McLeod he was by no means a stranger, having had occasion more than once to deal with him, boy as he was, for complications with riotous misdoings. He had happened to know, also, that it was Archie McLeod who had been head and front of the last year's revolt in the school, - the one boy that no teacher hitherto had been able to control. And here stood Archie McLeod, rising in his place, leader of the form, glancing down on the boys around him with the eye of a general, watching the teacher's eye, meanwhile, as a dog watches for his master's signal.

And the orderly yet alert and joyously eager expression of the whole school, - it had so much the look of a miracle to Sandy Bruce's eye, that, not having been for years accustomed to the restraint and dignity of school visitors, of technical official, he was on the point of giving a loud whistle of astonishment Luckily recollecting himself in time, he smothered the whistle and the "Whew! what's all this?" which had been on his tongue's end, in a vigorous and unnecessary blowing of his nose. And before that was over, and his eyes well wiped, there stood the whole school on its feet before him, and the room ringing with such a chorus as was never heard in a Prince Edward Island school-room before. This completed his bewilderment, and swallowed it up in delight. If Sandy Bruce had an overmastering passion in his rugged nature, it was for music. To the sound of the bag-pipes he had often said he would march to death and "not know it for dyin'." The drum and the fife could draw him as quickly now as when he was a boy, and the sweet singing of a woman's voice was all the token he wanted of the certainty of heaven and the existence of angels.

When Little Bel's clear, flute-like soprano notes rang out, carrying along the fifty young voices she led, Sandy jumped up on his feet, waving his hand, in a sudden heat of excitement, right and left; and looking swiftly all about him on the platform, he said: "It's not sittin' we'es take such welcome as this, my neebors!" Each man and woman there, catching the quick contagion, rose; and it was a tumultuous crowd of glowing faces that pressed forward around the piano as the singing went on, - fathers, mothers, rustics, all; and the children, pleased and astonished, sang better than ever, and when the chorus was ended it was some minutes before all was quiet.

Many things had been settled in that few minutes. John McDonald's heart was at rest. "The music'll carry a' before it, no matter if they do make a failure here 'n' there," he thought. "The bairn is a' right." The mother's heart was at rest also.

"She's done wonders wi' 'em, - wonders! I doubt not but it'll go through as it's begun. Her face's a picture to look on. Bless her!" Isabella was saying behind her placid smile.

"Eh, but she's won her guineas out o' us," thought old Dalgetty, ungrudgingly, "and won 'em well."

"I don't see why everybody is so afraid of Sandy Bruce," thought Little Bel. "He looks as kind and as pleased as my own father. I don't believe he'll ask any o' his botherin' questions."

What Sandy Bruce thought it would be hard to tell; nearer the truth, probably, to say that his head was in too much of a whirl to think anything. Certain it is that he did not ask any botherin' questions, but sat, leaning forward on his stout oaken staff, held firmly between his knees, and did not move for the next hour, his eyes resting alternately on the school and on the young teacher, who, now that her first fright was over, was conducting her entertainment with the composure and dignity of an experienced instructor.

The exercises were simple, - declamations, reading of selected compositions, examinations of the principal classes. At short intervals came songs to break the monotony. The first one after the opening chorus was "Banks and Braes of Bonnie Doon." At the first bars of this Sandy Bruce could not keep silence, but broke into a lone accompaniment in a deep bass voice, untrained but sweet.

"Ah," thought Little Bel, "what'll he say to the last one, I wonder?"

When the time came she found out. If she had chosen the arrangement of her music with full knowledge of Sandy Bruce's preferences, and with the express determination to rouse him to a climax of enthusiasm, she could not have done better.

When the end of the simple programme of recitations and exhibition had been reached, she came forward to the edge of the platform - her cheeks were deep pink now, and her eyes shone with excitement - and said, turning to the trustees and spectators: "We have finished, now, all we have to show for our year's work, and we will close our entertainment by singing 'Scots wha ha' wi' Wallace bled!'"

"Ay, ay! that wi' we!" shouted Sandy Bruce, again

leaping to his feet; and as the first of the grand chords of that grand old tune rang out full and loud under Little Bel's firm touch, he strode forward to the piano, and with a kindly nod to her struck in.

With the full force of his deep, bass-like, violoncello notes, gathering up all the others and fusing them into a pealing strain, it was electin'. Everybody sang. Old voices, that had not sung for a quarter of a century or more, joined in. It was a furor: Dalgetty swung his tartan cap, Sandy his hat; handkerchiefs were waved, staves rang on the floor. The children, half frightened in spite of their pleasure, were quieter than their elders.

"Eh, but it was good fun to see the old folks gone crazy for once!" said Archie McLeod, in recounting the scene. "Now, if they'd get that way oftener they'd not be so hard down on us youngsters."

At the conclusion of the song the first thing Little Bel heard was Dalgetty's piping voice behind her, -

"And guineas it is, Miss McDonald. Ye've won it fair an' square. Guineas it is!"

"Eh, what? Guineas! What is 't ye're sayin'?" asked Sandy Bruce; his eyes, steady glowing like coals, gazing at Little Bel.

"The supplement, sir," answered Little Bel, lifting her eyes roguishly to his. "Mr. Dalgetty thought I was too young for the school, an' he'd promise me no supplement till he saw if I'd be equal to 't."

This was the sly Bel's little revenge on Dalgetty, who began confusedly to explain that it was not he any more than the other trustees, and he only wished that they had all been here to see, as he had seen, how finely the school had been managed; but nobody heard what he said, for above all the humming and buzzing and laughing there came up from the centre of the school-room a reiterated call of "Sirs!" "Trustees!" "Mr. Trustee!" "Board!"

It was Archie McLeod, standing up on the backs of two seats, waving a white paper, and trying frantically to make himself heard. The face of a man galloping for life and death, coming up at the last second with a reprieve for one about to be shot, could hardly be fuller of intense anxiety than was Archie's as he waved his paper and shouted.

Little Bel gazed bewilderingly at him. This was not down on her programme of the exercises. What could it be?

As soon as partial silence enabled him to speak, Archie proceeded to read a petition, setting forth, to the respected Board of Trustees, that the undersigned, boys and girls of the Wissan Bridge School, did hereby unanimously request that they might have no other teacher than Miss McDonald, "as long as she lives."

This last clause had been the cause of bitter disputing between Archie and Sandy, - Sandy insisting upon having it in; Archie insisting that it was absurd, because they would not go to school as long as Miss McDonald lived. "But there's the little ones and the babies that'll be growin' up," retorted Sandy, "an' there'll never be another like her: I say, 'as long as she lives'"; and "as long as she lives" it was. And when Archie, with an unnecessary emphasis, delivered this closing clause of the petition, it was received with a roar of laughter from the platform, which made him flush angrily, and say, with a vicious punch in Sandy's ribs: "There, I told ye, it spoiled it a'. They're fit to die over it; an' sma' blame to 'em, ye silly!"

But he was reassured when he heard Sandy Bruce's voice overtopping the tumult with: "A vary sensible request, my lad; an' I, for one, am o' yer way o' thinkin'."

In which speech was a deeper significance than anybody at the time dreamed. In that hurly-burly and hilarious confusion no one had time to weigh words or note meanings; but there were some who recalled it a few months later when they were bidden to a wedding at the house of John McDonald, - a wedding at which Sandy Bruce was groom, and Little Bel the brightest, most winsome of brides.

It was an odd way that Sandy went to work to win her: his ways had been odd all his life, - so odd that it had long ago been accepted in the minds of the Charlottetown people that he would never find a woman to wed him; only now and then an unusually perspicacious person divined that the reason of his bachelorhood was not at all that women did not wish to wed him, spite of his odd ways, but that he himself found no woman exactly to his taste.

True it was that Sandy Bruce, aged forty, had never yet desired any woman for his wife till he looked into the face of Little Bel in the Wissan Bridge school-house. And equally true was it that before the last strains of "Scots wha ha' wi' Wallace bled" had died away on that memorable afternoon of her exhibition of her school, he had determined that his wife she should be.

This was the way he took to win her. No one can deny that it was odd.

There was some talk between him and his temporary colleague on the School Board, old Dalgetty, as they drove home together behind the brisk Norwegian ponies; and the result of this conversation was that the next morning early - in fact, before Little Bel was dressed, so late had she been indulged, for once, in sleeping, after her hard labors in the exhibition the day before - the Norwegian ponies were jingling their bells at John McDonald's door; and John himself might have been seen, with a seriously puzzled face, listening to words earnestly spoken by Sandy, as he shook off the snow and blanketed the ponies.

As the talk progressed, John glanced up involuntarily at Little Bel's window. Could it be that he sighed? At any rate, there was no regret in his heart as he shook Sandy's hand warmly, and said: "Ye've my free consent to try; but I doubt she's not easy won. She's her head now, an' her ain way; but she's a good lass, an' a sweet one."

"An' I need no man to tell me that," said the dauntless Sandy, as he gave back the hearty hand-grip of his friend; "an' she'll never repent it, the longest day o' her life, if she'll ha' me for her man." And he strode into the house, bearing in his hand the five golden guineas which his friend Dalgetty had, at his request, commissioned him to pay.

"Into her own hand, mind ye, mon," chuckled Dalgetty, mischievously. "Ye'll not be leavin' it wi' the mither." To which sly satire Sandy's only reply was a soft laugh and nod of his head.

As soon as Little Bel crossed the threshold of the room where Sandy Bruce stood waiting for her, she knew the errand on which he had come. It was written in his face. Neither could it be truthfully said to be a surprise to Little Bel; for she had not been woman, had she failed to recognize on the previous day that the rugged Scotchman's whole nature had gone out toward her in a sudden and overmastering attraction.

Sandy looked at her keenly. "Eh, ye know't a'ready," he said, - "the thing I came to say t' ye." And he paused, still eying her more like a judge than a lover.

Little Bel turned scarlet. This was not her ideal of a wooer. "Know what, Mr. Bruce?" she said resentfully. "How should I know what ye came to say?"

"Tush! tush, lass! do na prevaricate," Sandy began, his eyes gloating on her lovely confusion; "do na preteend - " But the sweet blue eyes were too much for him. Breaking down utterly, he tossed the guineas to one side on the table, and stretching out both hands toward Bel, he exclaimed, - "Ye're the sweetest thing the eyes o' a mon ever rested on, lass, an' I'm goin' to win ye if ye'll let me." And as Bel opened her mouth to speak, he laid one hand, quietly as a mother might, across her lips, and continued: "Na! na! I'll not let ye speak yet. I'm not a silly to look for ye to be ready to say me yes at this quick askin'; but I'll not let ye say me nay neither. Ye'll not refuse me the only thing I'm askin' the day, an' that's that ye'll let me try to make ye love me. Ye'll not say nay to that, lass. I'll gie my life to it." And now he waited for an answer.

None came. Tears were in Bel's eyes as she looked up in his face. Twice she opened her lips to speak, and twice her heart and the words failed her. The tears became drops and rolled down the cheeks. Sandy was dismayed.

"Ye're not afraid o' me, ye sweet thing, are ye?" he gasped out. "I'd not vex ye for the world. If ye bid me to go, I'd go."

"No, I'm not afraid o' ye, Mr. Bruce," sobbed Bel. "I don't know what it is makes me so silly. I'm not afraid o' ye, though. But I was for a few minutes yesterday," she added archly, with a little glint of a roguish smile, which broke through the tears like an April sun through rain, and turned Sandy's head in the twinkling of an eye.

"Ay, ay," he said; "I minded it weel, an' I said to myself then, in that first sight I had o' yer face, that I'd not harm a hair o' yer head. Oh, my little lass, would ye gie me a kiss, - just one, to show ye're not afraid, and to gie me leave to try to win ye out o' likin' into lovin'?" he continued, drawing closer and bending toward her.

And then a wonderful thing happened. Little Bel, who, although she was twenty years old, and had by no means been without her admirers, had never yet kissed any man but her father and brothers, put up her rosy lips, as confidingly as a little child, to be kissed by this strange wooer, who wooed only for leave to woo.

"An' if he'd only known it, he might ha' asked a' he wanted then as well as later," said Little Bel, honestly avowing the whole to her mother. "As soon as he put his hands on me the very heart in me said he was my man for a' my life. An' there's no shame in it that I can see. If a man may love that way in the lighting of an eye, why may not a girl do the same? There's not one kind o' heart i' the breast of a man an' another kind i' the breast of a woman, as ever I heard." In which Little Bel, in her innocence, was wiser than people wiser than she.

And after this there is no need of telling more, - only a picture or two which are perhaps worth sketching in few words. One is the expression which was seen on Sandy Bruce's face one day, not many weeks after his first interview with Little Bel, when, in reply to his question, "An' now, my own lass, what'll ye have for your weddin' gift from me? Tell me the thing ye want most i' a' the earth, an' if it's in my means ye shall have it the day ye gie me the thing I want maist i' the whole earth."

"I've got it a'ready, Sandy," said Little Bel, taking his face in her hands, and making a feint of kissing him; then withdrawing coquettishly. Wise, innocent Bel! Sandy understood.

"Ay, my lass; but next to me. What's the next thing ye'd have?"

Bel hesitated. Even to her wooer's generosity it might seem a daring request, - the thing she craved.

"Tell me, lass," said Sandy, sternly. "I've mair money than ye think. There's no lady in a' Charlottetown can go finer than ye if ye've a mind."

"For shame, Sandy!" cried Bel. "An' you to think it

was fine apparel I'd be askin'! It's a - a" - the word refused to leave her tongue - "a - piano, Sandy;" and she gazed anxiously at him. "I'll never ask ye for another thing till the day o' my death, Sandy, if ye'll gie me that."

Sandy shouted in delight. For a brief space a fear had seized him - of which he now felt shame indeed - that his sweet lassie might be about to ask for jewels or rich attire; and it would have sorely hurt Sandy's pride in her had this been so.

"A piano!" he shouted. "An' did ye not think I'd that a'ready in my mind? O' coorse, a piano, an' every other instrument under the skies that ye'll wish, my lass, ye shall have. The more music ye make, the gladder the house'll be. Is there nothin' else ye want, lass, - nothin'?"

"Nothing in all this world, Sandy, but you and a piano," replied Little Bel.

The other picture was on a New Year's Day, just a twelvemonth from the day of Little Bel's exhibition in the Wissan Bridge school-house. It is a bright day; the sleighing is superb all over the island, and the Charlottetown streets are full of gay sleighs and jingling bells, - none so gay, however, as Sandy Bruce's, and no bells so merry as the silver ones on his fierce little Norwegian ponies, that curvet and prance, and are all their driver can hold. Rolled up in furs to her chin, how rosy and handsome looks Little Bel by her husband's side, and how full of proud content is his face as he sees the people all turning to look at her beauty! And who is this driving the Norwegian ponies? Who but Archie, - Archie McLeod, who has followed his young teacher to her new home, and is to grow up, under Sandy Bruce's teachings, into a sharp and successful man of the shipping business.

And as they turn a corner they come near running into another fur-piled, swift-gliding sleigh, with a grizzled old head looking out of a tartan hood, and eyes like hawks', - Dalgetty himself; and as they pass the head nods and the eyes laugh, and a sharp voice cries, "Guineas it is!"

"Better than guineas!" answered back Mrs. Sandy Bruce, quick as a flash; and in the same second cries Archie, from the front seat, with a saucy laugh, "And as long as she lives, Mr. Dalgetty!"

The Captain of the "Heather Bell".

You might have known he was a Scotchman by the name of his little steamer; and if you had not known it by that, you would have known it as soon as you looked at him. Scotch, pure, unmitigated, unmistakable Scotch, was Donald Mackintosh, from the crown of his auburn head down to the soles of his big awkward feet. Six feet two inches in his stockings he stood, and so straight that he looked taller even than that; blue-gray eyes full of a canny twinkle; freckles, - yes, freckles that were really past the bounds of belief, for up into his hair they ran, and to the rims of his eyes, - no pale, dull, equivocal freckles, such as might be mistaken for dingy spots of anything else, but brilliant, golden-brown freckles, almost auburn like his hair. Once seen, never to be forgotten were Donald Mackintosh's freckles. All this does not sound like the description of a handsome man; but we are not through yet with what is to be said about Donald Mackintosh's looks. We have said nothing of his straight massive nose, his tawny curling beard, which shaded up to yellow around a broad and laughing mouth, where were perpetually flashing teeth of an even ivory whiteness a woman might have coveted. No, not handsome, but better than handsome, was Donald Mackintosh; he was superb. Everybody said so: nobody could have been found to dispute it, - nobody but Donald himself; he thought, honestly thought, he was hideous. All that he could see on the rare occasions when he looked in a glass was an expanse of fiery red freckles, topped off with what he would have called a shock of red hair. Uglier than anything he had ever seen in his life, he said to himself many a time, and grew shyer and shyer and more afraid of women each time he said it; and all this while there was not a girl in Charlottetown that did not know him in her thoughts, if indeed she did not openly speak of him, as that "splendid Donald Mackintosh," or "the handsome 'Heather Bell' captain."

But nothing could have made Donald believe this, which was in one way a pity, though in another way not. If he had known how women admired him, he would have inevitably been more or less spoiled by it, wasted his time, and not have been so good a sailor. On the other hand, it was a pity to see him, - forty years old, and alone in the world, - not a chick nor a child of his own, nor any home except such miserable makeshifts as a sailor finds in inns or boarding-houses.

It was a wonder that the warm-hearted fellow had kept a cheery nature and face all these years living thus. But the "Heather Bell" stood to him in place of wife, children, home. There is no passion in life so like the passion of a man for a woman as the passion of a sailor for his craft; and this passion Donald had to the full. It was odd how he came to be a born sailor. His father and his father's fathers, as far back as they knew, had been farmers - three generations of them - on the Prince Edward Island farm where Donald was born; and still more generations of them in old Scotland. Pure Scotch on both sides of the house for hundreds of years were the Mackintoshes, and the Gaelic tongue was to-day freer spoken in their houses than English.

The Mackintosh farm on Prince Edward Island was in the parish of Orwell Head, and Donald's earliest transgressions and earliest pleasures were runaway excursions to the wharves of that sleepy shore. To him Spruce Wharf was a centre of glorious maritime adventure. The small sloops that plied up and down the coast of the island, running in at the inlets, and stopping to gather up the farmers' produce and take it to Charlottetown markets, seemed to him as grand as Indiamen; and when, in his twelfth year, he found himself launched in life as a boy-of-all-work on one of these sloops, whose captain was a friend of his father's, he felt that his fortune was made. And so it was. He was in the line of promotion by virtue of his own enthusiasm. No plank too small for the born sailor to swim by. Before Donald was twenty-five he himself commanded one of these little coasting-vessels. From this he took a great stride forward, and became first officer on the iron-clad steamer plying between Charlottetown and the mainland. The winter service on this boat was terrible, - ploughing and cutting through nearly solid ice for long days and nights of storm. Donald did not like it. He felt himself lost out in the wild channel. His love was for the water near shore, - for the bays, inlets, and river-mouths he had known since he was a child.

He began to think he was not so much of a sailor as he had supposed, - so great a shrinking grew up in him winter after winter from the perils and hardships of the mail-steamer's route. But he persevered and bided his time, and in ten years had the luck to become owner and master of a trim little coasting-steamer which had been known for years as the "Sally Wright," making two trips a week from Charlottetown to Orwell Head, - known as the "Sally Wright" no longer, however; for the first thing Donald did was to repaint her, from stem to stern, white, with green and pink stripes, on her prow a cluster of pink heather blossoms, and "Heather Bell" in big letters on the side.

When he was asked where he got this fancy name, he said, lightly, he did not know; it was a good Scotch name. This was not true. Donald knew very well. On the window-sill in his mother's kitchen had stood always a pot of pink heather. Come summer, come winter, the place was never without a young heather growing; and the dainty pink bells were still to Donald the man, as they had been to Donald the child, the loveliest flowers in the world. But he would not for the profits of many a trip have told his comrade captains why he had named his boat the "Heather Bell." He had a sentiment about the name which he himself hardly understood. It seemed out of all proportion to the occasion; but a day was coming when it would seem more like a prophecy than a mere sentiment. He had builded better than he knew when he chose that name for the thing nearest his heart.

Charlottetown is not a gay place; its standards and methods of amusement are simple and primitive. Among the summer pleasures of the young people picnics still rank high, and picnic excursions by steamboat or sloop highest of all. Through June and July hardly a daily newspaper can be found which does not contain the advertisement of one or more of these excursions. After Donald made his little boat so fresh and gay with the pink and green colors, and gave her the winning new name, she came to be in great demand for these occasions.

How much the captain's good looks had to do with the

"Heather Bell's" popularity as a pleasure-boat it would not do to ask; but there was reason enough for her being liked aside from that. Sweet and fresh in and out, with white deck, the chairs and settees all painted green, and a gay streamer flying, - white, with three green bars, - and "Donald Mackintosh, Captain," in green letters, and below these a spray of pink heather, she looked more like a craft for festive sailing than for cruising about from one farm-landing to another, picking up odds and ends of farm produce, - eggs and butter, and oats and wool, - with now and then a passenger. Donald liked this slow cruising and the market-work best; but the picnic parties were profitable, and he took them whenever he could. He kept apart, however, from the merry-makers as much as possible, and was always glad at night when he had landed his noisy cargo safe back at the Charlottetown piers.

This disposition on his part to hold himself aloof was greatly irritating to the Charlottetown girls, and to no one of them so much as to pretty Katie McCloud, who, because she was his second cousin and had known him all her life, felt, and not without reason, that he ought to pay her something in the shape or semblance of attention when she was on board his boat, even if she were a member of a large and gay party, most of whom were strangers to him. There was another reason, too; but Katie had kept it so long locked in the bottom of her heart that she hardly realized its force and cogency, and, if she had, would have laughed, and put it as far from her thoughts as she could.

The truth was, Katie had been in love with Donald ever since she was ten years old and he was twenty, - a long time, seeing that she was now thirty and he forty; and never once, either in their youth or their middle age, had there been a word of love-making between them. All the same, deep in her heart the good little Katie had kept the image of Donald in sacred tenderness by itself. No other man's love-making, however earnest, - and Katie had been by no means without lovers, - had so much as touched this sentiment. She judged them all by this secret standard, and found them all wanting. She did not pine, neither did she take a step of forwardness, or even coquettish advance, to Donald. She was too full of Scotch reticence for that. The only step she did take, in hope of bringing him nearer to her, was the going to Charlottetown to learn the milliner's trade.

Poor Katie! if she had but known she threw away her last chance when she did it. She reasoned that Donald was in Charlottetown far more than he was anywhere else; that if she stayed at home on the farm she could see him only by glimpses, when the "Heather Bell" ran in at their landing, - in and out and off again in an hour. What was that? And maybe a Sunday once or twice a year, and at a Christmas gathering. No wonder Katie thought that in the town where his business lay and he slept three nights a week she would have a far better chance; that he would be glad to come and see her in her tidy little shop. But when Donald heard what she had done, he said gruffly: "Just like the rest; all for ribbons and laces and silly gear. I thought Katie'd more sense. Why didn't she stay at home on the farm?" And he said as much to her when he first saw her in her new quarters. She tried to explain to him that she wanted to support herself, and she could not do it on the farm.

"No need, - no need," said her relentless cousin; "there was plenty for all on the farm." And all the while he stood glowering at the counter spread with gay ribbons and artificial flowers, and Katie was ready to cry. This was in the first year of her life in Charlottetown. She was only twenty-two then. In the eight years since then matters had quieted down with Katie. It seemed certain that Donald would never marry. Everybody said so. And if a man had lived till forty without it, what else could be expected? If Katie had seen him seeking other women, her quiet and unrewarded devotion would no doubt have flamed up in jealous pain. But she knew that he gave to her as much as he gave to any, - occasional and kindly courtesy, no less, no more.

So the years slipped by, and in her patient industry Katie forgot how old she was growing, until suddenly, on her thirtieth birthday, something - the sight of a deepened line on her face, perhaps, or a pang of memory of the old childish past, such as birthdays always bring - something smote her with a sudden consciousness that life itself was slipping away, and she was alone. No husband, no child, no home, except as she earned each month, by fashioning bonnets and caps for the Charlottetown women, money enough to pay the rent of the two small rooms in which she slept, cooked, and plied her trade. Some tears rolled down Katie's face as she sat before her looking-glass thinking these unwelcome thoughts.

"I'll go to the Orwell Head picnic to-morrow," she said to herself. "It's so near the old place perhaps Donald'll walk over home with me. It's long since he's seen the farm, I'll be bound."

Now, Katie did not say to herself in so many words, "It will be like old times when we were young, and it may be something will stir in Donald's heart for me at the sight of the fields." Not only did she not say this; she did not know that she thought it; but it was there, all the same, a lurking, newly revived, vague, despairing sort of hope. And because it was there she spent half the day retrimming a bonnet and washing and ironing a gown to wear to the picnic; and after long and anxious pondering of the matter, she deliberately took out of her best box of artificial flowers a bunch of white heather, and added it to the bonnet trimming. It did not look overmuch like heather, and it did not suit the bonnet, of which Katie was dimly aware; but she wanted to say to Donald, "See, I put a sprig of heather in my bonnet in honor of your boat to-day." Simple little Katie!

It was a large and noisy picnic, of the very sort Donald most disliked, and he kept himself out of sight until the last moment, just before they swung round at Spruce Wharf. Then, as he stood on the upper deck giving orders about the flinging out of the ropes, Katie looked up at him from below, and called, in a half-whisper: "Oh, Donald, I was thinking I'd walk over home instead of staying here to the dance. Wouldn't ye be goin' with me, Donald? They'd be glad to see ye."

"Ay, Katie," answered Donald; "that will I, and be glad to be out of this." And as soon as the boat was safely moored, he gave his orders to his mate for the day, and leaping down joined the glad Katie; and before the picnickers had even missed them they were well out of sight, walking away briskly over the brown fields.

Katie was full of happiness. As she glanced up into Donald's face she found it handsomer and kinder than she had seen it, she thought, for many years.

"It was for this I came, Donald," she said merrily. "When I heard the dance was to be in the Spruce Grove I made up my mind to come and surprise the folks. It's nigh six months since I've been home."

"Pity ye ever left it, my girl," said Donald, gravely. "The home's the place for women." But he said it in a pleasant tone, and his eyes rested affectionately on Katie's face.

"Eh, but ye're bonny to-day, Katie; do ye know it?" he continued, his glance lingering on her fresh color and her smiling face. In his heart he was saying: "An' what is it makes her so young-looking to-day? It was an old face she had on the last time I saw her."

Happiness, Donald, happiness! Even those few minutes of it had worked the change.

Encouraged by this praise, Katie said, pointing to the flowers in her bonnet, "It's the heather ye're meanin', maybe, Donald, an' not me?"

"An' it's not," he replied earnestly, almost angrily, with a scornful glance at the flowers. "Ye'll not be callin' that heather. Did ye never see true heather, Katie? It's no more like the stalks ye've on yer head than a barrow's like my boat yonder."

Which was not true: the flowers were of the very best ever imported into Charlottetown, and were a better representation of heather than most artificial flowers are of the blossoms whose names they bear. Donald was not a judge; and if he had been, it was a cruel thing to say. Katie's eyes drooped: she had made a serious sacrifice in putting so dear a bunch of flowers on her bonnet, - a bunch that she had, in her own mind, been sure Lady Gownas, of Gownas House, would buy for her summer bonnet. She had made this sacrifice purely to please Donald, and this was what had come of it. Poor Katie! However, nothing could trouble her long to-day, with Donald by her side in the sunny, bright fields; and she would have him to herself till four in the afternoon.

As they drew near the farm-house a strange sound fell on their ears; it was as if a million of beehives were in full blast of buzzing in the air. At the same second both Donald and Katie paused, listening. "What can that be, now?" exclaimed Donald. Before the words had left his lips, Katie cried, "It's a bee! - Elspie's spinning-bee."

The spinning-bees are great fêtes among the industrious maidens of Prince Edward Island. After the spring shearings are over, the wool washed and carded and made into rolls, there begin to circulate invitations to spinning-bees at the different farm-houses. Each girl carries her spinning-wheel on her shoulder. By eight o'clock in the morning all are gathered and at work: some of them have walked ten miles or more, and barefoot too, their shoes slung over the shoulder with the wheel. Once arrived, they waste no time. The rolls of wool are piled high in the corners of the rooms, and it is the ambition of each one to spin all she can before dark. At ten o'clock cakes and lemonade are served; at twelve, the dinner, - thick soup, roast meat, vegetables, coffee and tea, and a pudding. All are seated at a long table, and the hostesses serve; at six o'clock comes supper, and then the day's work is done; after that a little chat or a ramble over the farm, and at eight o'clock all are off for home. No young men, no games, no dances; yet the girls look forward to the bees as their greatest spring pleasures, and no one grudges the time or the strength they take.

It was, indeed, a big bee that Elspie McCloud was having this June morning. Twenty young girls, all in long white aprons, were spinning away as if on a wager when Donald and Katie appeared at the door. The door opened directly into the large room where they were. Katie went first, Donald hanging back behind. "I think I'll not go in," he was shamefacedly saying, and halting on the step, when above all the wheel-whirring and yarn-singing came a glad cry, -

"Why, there's Katie - Katie McCloud! and Donald Mackintosh! For pity's sake!" (the Prince Edward Islander's strongest ejaculation.) "Come in! come in!" And in a second more a vision, it seemed to the dazed Donald, - but it was not a vision at all, only a buxom young girl in a blue homespun gown, - had seized him with one hand and Katie with the other, and drawn them both into the room, into the general whir and *mêlée* of wheels, merry faces, and still merrier voices.

It was Elspie, Katie's youngest sister, - Katie's special charge and care when she was a baby, and now her special pet. The greatest desire of Katie's heart was to have Elspie with her in Charlottetown, but the father and mother would not consent.

Donald stood like a man in a dream. He did not know it; but from the moment his eyes first fell on Elspie's face they had followed it as iron follows the magnet. Were there ever such sweet gray eyes in the world? and such a pink and white skin? and hair yellow as gold? And what, oh, what did she wear tucked in at the belt of her white apron but a sprig of heather! Pink heather, - true, genuine, actual pink heather, such as Donald had not seen for many a year. No wonder the eyes of the captain of the "Heather Bell" followed that spray of pink heather wherever it went flitting about from place to place, never long in one, - for it was now time for dinner, and Donald and the old people were soon seated at a small table by themselves, not to embarrass the young girls, and Elspie and Katie together served the dinner; and though Elspie never once came to the small table, yet did Donald see every motion she made and hear every note of her lark's voice. He did not mistake what had happened to him. Middle-aged, inexperienced, sober-souled man as he was, he knew that at last he had got a wound, - a life wound, if it were not healed, - and the consciousness of it struck him more and more dumb, till his presence was like a damper on the festivities; so much so, that when at three in the afternoon he and Katie took their departure, the door had no more than closed on them before Elspie exclaimed pettishly: "An' indeed I wish Katie'd left Cousin Donald behind. I don't know what it is she thinks so much of him for. She's always sayin' there's none like him; an' it's lucky it's true. The great glowerin' steeple o' a man, with no word in his mouth!" And the young maidens all agreed with her. It was a strange thing for a man to come and go like that, with nothing to say for himself, they said, and he so handsome too.

"Handsome!" cried Elspie; "is it handsome, - the face all a spatter with the color of the hair? He's nice eyes of his own, but his skin's deesgustin'." Which speech, if Donald had overheard it, would have caused that there should never have been this story to tell. But luckily Donald did not. All that he bore away from the

McCloud farm-house that June morning was a picture of a face and flitting figure, and the sound in his ears of a voice, - a picture and a sound which he was destined to see and hear all his life.

He scarcely spoke on his way back to the boat, and Katie perplexed herself vainly trying to account for his silence. It must be, she thought, that he had been vexed by the sight of so many girls and the sound of their idle chatter. He would have liked it better if nobody but the family had been at home. What a shame for a man to live alone as he did, and get into such unsocial ways! He grew more and more averse to society each year. Now, if he were only married, and had a bright home, where people came and went, with a bit of a tea now and then, how good it would be for him, - take the stiffness out of his ways, and make him more as he used to be fifteen, or even ten years ago! And so the good Katie went on in her placid mind, trotting along silently by his side, waiting for him to speak.

"Where did she get the heather?"

"What!" exclaimed Katie. The irrelevant question sounded like the speech of one talking in his sleep. "Oh," she continued, "ye mean Elspie!"

"Ay," said Donald. "She'd a bit of heather in her belt, - the true heather, not sticks like yon," pointing a contemptuous finger toward Katie's bonnet. "Where did she get it?"

"Mother's always the heather growing in the house," answered Katie. "She says she's homesick unless she sees it. It was grandmother brought it over in the first, and it's never been let die out."

"My mother the same," said Donald. "It's the first blossom I remember, an' I'm thinking it will be the last," he continued, gazing at Katie absently; but his face did not look as if it were absently he gazed. There was a glow on his cheeks, and an intense expression in his eyes which Katie had never seen there. They warmed her heart.

"Yes," she said, "one can never forget what one has loved in the youth."

"True, Katie, true. There's nothing like one's own and earliest," replied Donald, full of his new and thrilling emotion; and as he said it he reached out his hand and took hold of Katie's, as if they were boy and girl together. "Many's the time I've raced wi' ye this way, Katie," he said affectionately.

"Ay, when I was a wee thing; an' ye always let go my hand at last, and pretended I could outrin ye," laughed Katie, blissful tears filling her eyes.

What a happy day was this! Had it not been an inspiration to bring Donald back to the old farm-house? Katie was sure it had. She was filled with sweet reveries; and so silent on the way home that her merry friends joked her unmercifully about her long walk inland with the Captain.

It was late in the night, or rather it was early the next morning, when the "Heather Bell" reached her wharf.

"I'll go up with ye, Katie," said Donald. "It's not decent for ye to go alone."

And when he bade her good-night he looked

half-wistfully in her face, and said: "But it's a lonely house for ye to come to, Katie, an' not a soul but yourself in it." And he held her hand in his affectionately, as a cousin might.

Katie's heart beat like a hammer in her bosom at these words, but she answered gravely: "Yes, it was sorely lonely at first, an' I wearied myself out to get them to give me Elspie to learn the business wi' me; but I'm more used to it now."

"That is what I was thinkin'," said Donald, "that if the two o' ye were here together, ye'd not be so lonely. Would she not like to come?"

"Ay, that would she," replied the unconscious Katie; "she pines to be with me. I'm more her mother than the mother herself; but they'll never consent."

"She's bonny," said Donald. I'd not seen her since she was little."

"She's as good as she is bonny," said Katie, warmly; and that was the last word between Katie and Donald that night.

"As good as she is bonny." It rang in Donald's ears like a refrain of heavenly music as he strode away. "As good as she is bonny;" and how good must that be? She could not be as good as she was bonny, for she was the bonniest lass that ever drew breath. Gray eyes and golden hair and pink cheeks and pink heather all mingled in Donald's dreams that night in fantastic and impossible combinations; and more than once he waked in terror, with the sweat standing on his forehead from some nightmare fancy of danger to the

"Heather Bell" and to Elspie, both being inextricably entangled together in his vision.

The visions did not fade with the day. They pursued Donald, and haunted his down-sitting and his uprising. He tried to shake them off, drive them away; for when he came to think the thing over soberly, he called himself an old fool to be thus going daft about a child like Elspie.

"Barely twenty at the most, and me forty. She'd not look at an old fellow like me, and maybe't would be like a sin if she did," said Donaldto himself over and over again. But it did no good. "As good as she is bonny, bonny, bonny," rang in his ears, and the blue eyes and golden hair and merry smile floated before his eyes. There was no help for it. Since the world began there have been but two roads out of this sort of mystic maze in which Donald now found himself lost, - but two roads, one bright with joy, one dark with sorrow. And which road should it be Donald's fate to travel must be for the child Elspie to say. After a few days of bootless striving with himself, during which time he had spent more hours with Katie than he had for a year before, - it was such a comfort to him to see in her face the subtle likeness to Elspie, and to hear her talk about plans of bringing her to Charlottetown for a visit if nothing more, - after a few days of this, Captain Donald, one Saturday afternoon, sailing past Orwell Head, suddenly ran into the inlet where he had taken the picnic party, and, mooring the "Heather Bell" at Spruce Wharf, announced to his astonished mate that he should lie by there till Monday.

It was a bold step of Captain Donald's. But he was not a man for half-and-half ways in anything; and he had said grimly to himself that this matter must be ended one way or the other, - either he would win the child or lose her. He would know which. Girls had loved men twenty years older than themselves, and girls might again.

The Sunday passed off better than his utmost hopes. Everybody except Elspie was cordially glad to see him. Visitors were not so common at the Orwell Head farm-houses that they could fail of welcome. The McCloud boys were thankful to hear all that Donald had to tell, and with the old father and mother he had always been a prime favorite. It had been a sore disappointment to them, as year after year went by, to see that there seemed no likelihood of his becoming Katie's husband. As the day wore on, even Elspie relaxed a little from her indifferent attention to him, and began to perceive that, spite of the odious freckles, he was, as the girls had said, a handsome man.

Partly because of this, and partly from innate coquetry, she said, when he was taking leave, "Ye'll not be comin' again for another year, maybe?"

"Ye'll see, then!" laughed Donald, with a sudden wise impulse to refrain from giving the reply which sprang to his lips, - "To-morrow, if ye'd ask me!"

And from the same wise, strangely wise impulse he curbed his desire to go again the next Sunday and the next. Not until three weeks had passed did he go; and then Elspie was clearly and unmistakably glad to see him. This was all Donald wanted. "I'll win her, the bonny thing!" he said to himself. "An' I'll not be long, either."

And he was right. A girl would have been hard indeed that would not have been touched by the beaming, tender face which Donald wore, now that hope lighted it up. His masterful bearing, too, was a pleasure to the spirited Elspie, who had no liking for milksops, and had sent off more than one lover because he came crawling too humbly to her feet. Elspie had none of the gentle, quiet blood which ran in Katie's veins. She had even been called Firebrand in her younger, childish days, so hot was her temper, so hasty her tongue. But the firm rule of the Scottish household and the pressure of the stern Scotch Calvinism preached in their kirk had brought her well under her own control.

"Eh, but the bonny lass has hersel' well in hand," thought the admiring Donald more than once, as he saw her in some family discussion or controversy keep silence, with flushing cheeks, when sharp words rose to her tongue.

All this time Katie was plodding away at her millinery, inexpressibly cheered by Donald's new friendliness. He came often to see her, and told her with the greatest frankness of his visits at the farm. He would take her some day, he said; the trouble was, he could never be sure beforehand when it would answer for him to stop there. Katie sunned herself in this new familiar intercourse, and the thought of Donald running up to the old farm of a Sunday as if he were one of the brothers going home. In the contentment of these thoughts she grew younger and prettier, - began to look as she did at twenty. And Donald, gazing scrutinizingly in her face one day, seeking, as he was always doing, for stray glimpses of resemblance to Elspie, saw this change, and impulsively told her of it.

"But ye're growin' young, Katie - d'ye know it? - young and bonny, my girl."

And Katie listened to the words with such sweet joy she feared her face would tell too much, and put up her hands to hide it, crying: "Ah, ye're tryin' to make me silly, you Donald, with such flatterin'. We're gettin' old, Donald, you an' me," she added, with a guilty little undercurrent of thought in her mind. "D'ye mind that I was thirty last month?"

"Ay," replied Donald, gloomily, his face darkening, - "ay; I mind, by the same token, I'm forty. It's no need ye have to be callin' yersel' old. But I'm old, an' no mistake." The thought, as Katie had put it, had been gall and wormwood to him. If Katie thought him old, what must he seem to Elspie!

It was early in June that Elspie had had the spinning-bee to which Katie had brought the unwelcome Donald. The summer sped past, but a faster summer than any reckoned on the calendar of months and days was speeding in Elspie's heart. Such great love as Donald's reaches and warms its object as inevitably as the heat of a fire warms those near it. Early in June the spinning-bee, and before the last flax was pulled, early in September, Elspie knew that she was restless till Donald came, glad when he was by her side, and strangely sorry when he went away. Still, she was not ready to admit to herself that it was anything more than her natural liking for any pleasant friend who broke in on the lonely monotony of the farm life.

The final drying of the flax, which is an important crop on most of the Prince Edward Island farms, is put off until autumn. After its first drying in the fields where it grew, it is stored in bundles under cover till all the other summer work is done, and autumn brings leisure. Then the flax camp, as it is called, is built, - a big house of spruce boughs; walls, flat roof, all of the green spruce boughs, thick enough to keep out rain. This is usually in the heart of a spruce grove. Thither the bundles of flax are carried and stacked in piles. In the centre of the inclosure a slow fire is lighted, and above this on a frame of slats the stalks of flax are laid for their last drying. It is a difficult and dangerous process to keep the fire hot enough and not too hot, to shift and turn and lift the flax at the right moment. Sometimes only a sudden flinging of moist earth upon the fire saves it from blazing up into the flax, and sometimes one careless second's oversight loses the whole, - flax, spruce-bough house, all, in a light blaze, and gone in a breath.

The McClouds' flax camp had been built in the edge of the spruce grove where the picnickers had held their dance and merry-making on that June day, memorable to Donald and Elspie and Katie. It was well filled with flax, in the drying of which nobody was more interested than Elspie. She had big schemes for spinning and weaving in the coming winter. A whole piece of linen she had promised to Katie, and a piece for herself, and, as Elspie thought it over, maybe a good many more pieces than one she might require for herself before spring. Who knew?

It was October now, and many a Sunday evening had Elspie walked with Donald alone down to Spruce Wharf, and lingered there watching the last curl of steam from the "Heather Bell" as she rounded the point, bearing Donald away. Elspie could not doubt why Donald came. Soon she would wonder why he came and went so many times silent; that is, silent in words, eloquent of eye and hand, - even the touch of his hand was like a promise.

No one was defter and more successful in this handling of the flax over the fire than Elspie. It had sometimes happened that she, with the help of one brother, had dried the whole crop. It was not thought safe for one person to work at it alone for fear of accident with the fire. But it fell out on this October afternoon, a Saturday, that Elspie, feeling sure of Donald's being on his way to spend the Sunday with her, had walked down to the wharf to meet him. Seeing no signs of the boat, she went back to the flax camp, lighted the fire, and began to spread the flax on the slats. There was not much more left to be dried, - "not more than three hours' work in all," she said to herself. "Eh, but I'd like to have done with it before the Sabbath!" And she fell to work with a will, so briskly to work that she did not realize how time was flying, - did not, strangest of all, hear the letting off of steam when the "Heather Bell" moored at the wharf; and she was still busily turning and lifting and separating the stalks of flax, bending low over the frame, heated, hurrying, her whole heart in her work, when Donald came striding up the field from the wharf, - striding at his greatest pace, for he was disturbed at not finding Elspie at the landing to meet him. He turned his head toward the spruce grove, thinking vaguely of the June picnic, and what had come of his walking away from the dance that morning, when suddenly a great column of smoke and fire rolled up from the grove, and in the same second came piercing shrieks in Elspie's voice. The grove was only a few rods away, but it seemed to Donald an eternity before he reached the spot, to see not only the spruce boughs and flax on fire, but Elspie tossing up her arms like one crazed, her gown all ablaze. The brave, foolish girl, at the first blazing of the stalks on the slats, had darted into the corner of the house and snatched an armful of the piled flax there to save it; but as she passed the flaming centre the whole sheaf she carried had caught fire also, and in a twinkling of an eye had blazed up around her head, and when she dropped it, had blazed up again fiercer than ever around her feet.

With a groan Donald seized her. The flames leaped on him, too, as if to wrestle with him; his brown beard crackled, his hair, but he fought through it all. Throwing Elspie on the ground, he rolled her over and over, crying aloud, "Oh, my darlin', if I break your sweet bones, it is better than the fire!" And indeed it seemed as if it must break her bones, so fiercely he rolled her over and over, tearing off his woollen coat to smother the fire; beating it with his tartan cap, stamping it with his knees and feet "Oh, my darlin'! make yourself easy. I'll save ye! I'll save ye if I die for it," he cried.

And through the smoke and the fire and the terror Elspie answered back: "I'll not leave ye, my Donald. We're gettin' it under." And with her own scorched hands she pulled the coat-flaps down over the smouldering bits of flax, and tore off her burning garments.

Not a coward thread in her whole body had little Elspie, and in less time than the story could ever be told, all was over, and safely; and there they sat on the ground, the two, locked in each other's arms, - Donald's beard gone, and much of his hair; Elspie's pretty golden hair also blackened, burned. It was the first thing Donald saw after he made sure danger was past. Laying his hand on her head, he said, with a half-sob, - he was hysterical now there was nothing more to be done: "Oh, your bonny hair, my darlin'! It's all scorched away."

"It'll grow!" said Elspie, looking up in his eyes archly. Her head was on his shoulder, and she nestled closer; then she burst into tears and laughter together, crying: "Oh, Donald, it was for you I was callin'. Did ye hear me? I said to myself when the fire took hold, 'O God, send Donald to save me!'"

"An' he sent me, my darlin'," answered Donald. "Ye are my own darlin'; say it, Elspie, say it!" he continued. "Oh, ye bonny bairn, but I've loved ye like death since the first day I set eyes on your bonny face! Say ye're my darlin'!"

But he knew it without her saying a word; and the whispered "Yes, Donald, I'm your darlin' if you want me," did not make him any surer.

There was a great outcrying and trembling of hearts at the farm-house when Donald and Elspie appeared in this sorry plight of torn and burned clothes, blackened faces, scorched and singed hair. But thankfulness soon swept away all other emotions, - thankfulness and a great joy, too; for Donald's second word was, turning to the old father: "An' it is my own that I've saved; she's gien hersel' to me for all time, an' we'll ask for your blessin' on us without any waitin'!" Tears filled the mother's eyes. She thought of another daughter. A dire instinct smote her of woe to Katie.

"Ay, Donald," she said, "it's a good day to us to see ye

Helen Hunt Jackson

enter the house as a son; but I never thought o' - " She stopped.

Donald's quick consciousness imagined part of what she had on her mind. "No," he said, half sad in the midst of his joy, "o' course ye didn't; an' I wonder at mysel'. It's like winter weddin' wi' spring, ye'll be sayin'. But I'll keep young for her sake. Ye'll see she's no old man for a husband. There's nothing in a' the world I'll not do for the bairn. It's no light love I bear her."

"Ye'll be tellin' Katie on the morrow?" said the unconscious Elspie.

"Ay, ay," replied the equally unconscious Donald; "an' she'll be main glad o' 't. It's a hundred times in the summer that she's been sayin' how she longed to have you in the town wi' her. An' now ye're comin', comin' soon, oh, my bonny. I'll make a good home for ye both. Katie's the same's my own, too, for always."

The mother gazed earnestly at Donald. Could it be that he was so unaware of Katie's heart? "Donald," she said suddenly, "I'll go down wi' ye if ye'll take me. I've been wantin' to go. There's a many things I've to do in the town."

It had suddenly occurred to her that she might thus save Katie the shock of hearing the news first from Donald's lips.

It was well she did. When, with stammering lips and she hardly knew in what words, she finally broke it to Katie that Donald had asked Elspie to be his wife, and that Elspie loved him, and they would soon be married,

Katie stared into her face for a moment with wide, vacant eyes, as if paralyzed by some vision of terror. Then, turning white, she gasped out, "Mother!" No word more. None was necessary.

"Ay, my bairn, I know," said the mother, with a trembling voice; "an' I came mysel' that no other should tell ye."

A long silence followed, broken only by an occasional shuddering sigh from Katie; not a tear in her eyes, and her cheeks as scarlet as they had been white a few moments before. The look on her face was terrifying.

"Will it kill ye, bairn?" sobbed the mother at last. "Don't look so. It must be borne, my bairn; it must be borne."

It was a shrill voice, unlike Katie's, which replied: "Ay, I'll bear it; it must be borne. There's none knows it but you, mother," she added, with a shade of relief in the tone.

"An' never will if ye're brave, bairn," answered the mother.

"It was the day of the picnic," cried Katie; "was't not? I remember he said she was bonny."

"Ay, 'twas then," replied the mother, so sorely torn between her love for the two daughters, between whom had fallen this terrible sword. "Ay, it was then. He says she has not been out of his mind by the night or by the day since it."

Katie shivered. "And it was I brought him," she said,

Helen Hunt Jackson

with a tearless sob bitterer than any loud weeping. "Ye'll be goin' back the night?" she added drearily.

"I'll bide if ye want me," said the mother.

"I'm better alone, mother," said Katie, her voice for the first time faltering. "I'll bear it. Never fear me, mother; but I'm best alone for a bit. Ye'll give my warm love to Elspie, an' send her down here to me to stay till she's married. I'll help her best if she's here. There'll be much to be done. I'll do 't, mother; never fear me."

"Are ye countin' too much on yer strength, bairn?" asked the now weeping mother. "I'd rather see ye give way like."

"No, no," cried Katie, impatiently. "Each one has his own way, mother; let me have mine. I'll work for Donald and Elspie all I can. Ye know she was always like my own bairn more than a sister. The quicker she comes the better for me, mother. It'll be all over then. Eh, but she'll be a bonny bride!" And at these words Katie's tears at last flowed.

"There, there, bairn! Have out the tears; they're healin' to grief," exclaimed her mother, folding her arms tight around her and drawing her head down on her shoulder as she had done in her babyhood.

Katie was right. When she had Elspie by her side, and was busily at work in helping on all the preparations for the wedding, the worst was over. There was a strange blending of pang and pleasure in the work. Katie wondered at herself; but it grew clearer and clearer to her each day that since Donald could not be hers she was glad he was Elspie's. "If he'd married a stranger it would ha' broke my heart far worse, far worse," she said many a time to herself as she sat patiently stitching, stitching, on Elspie's bridal clothes. "He's my own in a way, after a', so long's he's my brother. There's nobody can rob me o' that." And the sweet light of unselfish devotion beamed more and more in her countenance, till even the mother that bore her was deceived, and said in her heart that Katie could not have been so very much in love with Donald after all.

There was one incident which for a few moments sorely tested Katie's self-control. The spray of white heather blossom which she had worn to the June picnic she had on the next day put back in her box of flowers for sale, hoping that she might yet find a customer for it. The delicate bells were not injured either in shape or color. It was a shame to lose it for one day's wear, thought the thrifty Katie; and most surely she herself would never wear it again. She could not even see it without a flush of mortification as she recalled Donald's contempt for it. The privileged Elspie, rummaging among all Katie's stores, old and new, spied this white heather cluster one day, and snatching it up exclaimed: "The very thing for my weddin' bonnet, Katie! I'll have it in. The bride o' the master o' the 'Heather Bell' should be wed with the heather bloom on her."

Katie's face flushed. "It's been worn, Elspie," she said; "I had it in a bonnet o' my own. Don't ye remember I wore it to the picnic? an' then it didna suit, an' I put it back in the box. It's not fit for ye. I've a bunch o' lilies o' the valley, better."

"No; I'll have this," pursued Elspie. "It's as white's the

driven snow, an' not hurt at all. I'm sure Donald'll like it better than all the other flowers i' the town."

"Indeed, then, he won't," said Katie, sharply; on which Elspie turned upon her with a flashing eye, and said, -

"An' which 'll be knowin' best, do ye think? What is it ye mean?"

"Nothing," said Katie, meekly; "only he said, that day I'd the bonnet on, it was no more than sticks, an' not like the true heather at all."

"All he knows, then! Ye'll see he'll not say it looks like sticks when it's on the bonnet I'm goin' to church in," retorted Elspie, dancing to the looking-glass, and holding the white heather bells high up against her golden curls. "It's the only flower in all yer boxes I want, Katie, and ye'll not grudge it to me, will ye, dear?" And the sparkling Elspie threw herself on the floor by Katie, and flung her arms across her knees, looking up into her face with a wilful, loving smile.

"No wonder Donald loves her so, - the bonny thing!" thought Katie. "God knows I'd grudge ye nothing on earth, Elspie," she said, in a voice so earnest that Elspie looked wonderingly at her.

"Is it a very dear flower, sister?" she said penitently. "Does it cost too much money for Elspie?"

"No, bairn, it's not too dear," said Katie, herself again.

"The lilies were dearer. But ye'll have the heather an' welcome, if ye will; an' I doubt not it'll look all right in

Donald's eyes when he sees it this time."

It was indeed a good home that Donald made for his wife and her sister. He was better to do in worldly goods than they had supposed. His long years of seclusion from society had been years of thrift and prosperity. No more milliner-work for Katie. Donald would not hear of it. So she was driven to busy herself with the house, keeping from Elspie's willing and eager hands all the harder tasks, and laying up stores of fine-spun linen and wool for future use in the family. It was a marvel how content Katie found herself as the winter flew by. The wedding had taken place at Christmas, and the two sisters and Donald had gone together from the church to Donald's new house, where, in a day or two, everything had settled into peaceful grooves of simple, industrious habit, as if they had been there all their lives.

Donald's happiness was of the deep and silent kind. Elspie did not realize the extent of it. A freer-spoken, more demonstrative lover would have found heartier response and more appreciation from her. But she was a loyal, loving, contented little wife, and there could not have been found in all Charlottetown a happier household, to the eye, than was Donald's for the first three months after his marriage.

Then a cloud settled on it. For some inexplicable reason the blooming Elspie, who had never had a day's illness in her life, drooped in the first approach of the burden of motherhood. A strange presentiment also seized her. After the first brief gladness at the thought of holding a child of her own in her arms, she became overwhelmed with a melancholy certainty of her own death.

"I'll never live to see it, Katie," she said again and again. "It'll be your bairn, an' not mine. Ye'll never give it up, Katie? - promise me. Ye'll take care of it all your life? - promise." And Katie, terrified by her earnestness, promised everything she asked, all the while striving to reassure her that her fears were needless.

No medicines did Elspie good; mind and body alike reacted on each other; she failed hour by hour till the last; and when her time of trial came, the sad presentiment fulfilled itself, and she died in giving birth to her babe.

When Katie brought the child to the stunned and stricken Donald, saying, "Will ye not look at him, Donald? it is as fine a man-child's was ever seen," he pushed her away, saying in a hoarse whisper, -

"Never let me see its face. She said it was to be your bairn and not hers. Take it and go. I'll never look on it."

Donald was out of his reason when he spoke these words, and for long after. They bore with him tenderly and patiently, and did as they could for the best; Katie, the wan and grief-stricken Katie, being the chief adviser and planner of all.

Elspie's body was carried home and buried near the spruce grove, in a little copse of young spruces which Donald pointed out. This was the only wish he expressed about anything. Katie took the baby with her to the old homestead. She dared not try to rear it without her mothers help.

It was many months before Donald came to the farm. This seemed strange to all except Katie. To her it seemed the most natural thing, and she grew impatient with all who thought otherwise.

"I'd feel that way mysel'," she repeated again and again. "He'll come when he can, but it'll be long first. Ye none of ye know what a love it was he'd in his heart for Elspie."

When at last Donald came, the child, the little Donald, was just able to creep, - a chubby, blue-eyed, golden-haired little creature, already bearing the stamp and likeness of his mother's beauty.

At the first sight of his face Donald staggered, buried his head in his hands, and turned away. Then, looking again, he stretched out his arms, took the baby in them, and kissed him convulsively over and over. Katie stood by, looking on, silently weeping. "He's like her," she said.

"Ay," said Donald.

The healing had begun. "A little child shall lead them," is of all the Bible prophecies the one oftenest fulfilled. It soon grew to be Donald's chiefest pleasure to be with his boy, and he found more and more irksome the bonds of business which permitted him so few intervals of leisure to visit the farm. At last one day he said to Katie, -

"Katie, couldn't ye make your mind up to come up to Charlottetown? I'd get ye a good house, an' ye could have who ye'd like to live wi' ye. I'm like one hungry all the time I'm out o' reach o' the little lad."

Katie's eyes fell. She did not know what to reply.

"I do not know, Donald," she faltered. "It's hard for you having him away, but this is my home now, Donald. I've a dread o' leavin' it. And there is nobody I know who could come to live with me."

A strange thought shot through Donald's brain. "Katie," he said, then paused. Something in the tone startled Katie. She lifted her eyes; read in his the thought which had made the tone so significant to her ear.

Unconsciously she cried out at the sight, "Oh, Donald!"

"Ay, Katie," he said slowly, with a grave tenderness, "why might not I come and live wi' ye? Are ye not the mother o' my child? Did she not give him to ye with her own lips? An' how could ye have him without me? I think she must ha' meant it so. Let me come, Katie."

It was an unimpassioned wooing; but any other would have repelled Katie's sense of loyalty and truth.

"Have ye love for me, Donald?" she said searchingly.

"All the love left in me is for the little lad and for you, Katie," answered Donald. "I'll not deceive you, Katie. It's but a broken man I am; but I've always loved ye, Katie. I'll be a good man t' ye, lass. Come and be the little lad's mother, and let me live wi' my own once more. Will ye come?" As he said these words, he stretched out his arms toward Katie; and she, trembling, afraid to be glad, shadowed by the sad past, yet trusting in the future, crept into them, and was folded close to the heart she had so faithfully loved all her life.

"I promised Elspie," she whispered, "that I'd never, never give him to another."

"Ay," said Donald, as he kissed her. "He's your bairn, my Katie. Ye'll be content wi' me, Katie?"

"Yes, Donald, if I make you content," she replied; and a look of heavenly peace spread over her face.

The next morning Katie went alone to Elspie's grave. It seemed to her that only there could she venture to look her new future in the face. As she knelt by the low mound, her tears falling fast, she murmured, -

"Eh, my bonny Elspie, ye'd the best o' his love. But it's me that'll be doin' for him till I die, an' that's better than a' the love."

Dandy Steve.

Everything in this world is relative, and nothing more so than the significance of the same word in different localities. If Dandy Steve had walked Broadway in the same clothes which he habitually wore in the Adirondack wilderness, not only would nobody have called him a dandy, but every one would have smiled sarcastically at the suggestion of that epithet's being applied to him. Nevertheless, "Dandy Steve" was the name by which he was familiarly known all through the Saranac region; and judging by the wilderness standard, the adjective was not undeserved. No such flannel shirts, no such jaunty felt hats, no such neckties, had ever been worn by Adirondack guides as Dandy Steve habitually wore. And as for his buck-skin trousers, they would not have disgraced a Sioux chief, - always of the softest and yellowest skins, always daintily made, the seams set full of leather fringes, and sometimes marked by lines of delicate embroidery in white quills. There were those who said that Dandy Steve had an Indian wife somewhere on the Upper Saranac, but nobody knew; and it would have been a bold man who asked an intrusive question of Dandy Steve, or ventured on any impertinent jesting about his private affairs. Certain it was that none but Indian hands embroidered the fine buckskins he wore; but, then, there were such buckskins for sale, - perhaps he bought them. A man who would spend the money he did for neckties and fine flannel shirts would not stop at any extravagance in the price of trousers. The buckskins, however, were not the only evidence in this case. There was a well-authenticated tale of a brilliant red shawl - a woman's shawl - and a pair of silver bangles once seen in Dandy Steve's cabin. A man had gone in upon him suddenly one evening without the formality of knocking. Such foolish conventionalities were not in vogue on the Saranac; this was before Steve took to guiding. It was in the first year after he appeared in that region, while he was living like a hermit alone, or supposed to be alone, in a tiny log cabin on an island not much bigger than his cabin.

This man - old Ben, the oldest guide there - having been hindered at some of the portages, and finding himself too late to reach his destination that night, seeing the glimmer of light from Steve's cabin, had rowed to the island, landed, and, with the thoughtless freedom of the country, walked in at the half-open door.

He was fond of telling the story of his reception; and as he told it, it had a suspicious sound, and no mistake. Steve was sitting in a big arm-chair before his table; over the arm of the chair was flung the red shawl. On the table lay an open book and the silver bangles in it, as if some one had just thrown them off. At sound of entering footsteps Steve sprang up, with an angry oath, and hastily closing the book threw it and the bangles into the chair from which he had risen, then crowded the shawl down upon them into as small a compass as possible.

"His eyes blazed like lightnin', or sharper," said old Ben, "an' I declare t' ye I was skeered. Fur a minut I thought he was a loonatic, sure's death. But in a minut more he was all right, an' there couldn't nobody treat a feller handsomer than he did me that night an' the next mornin'; but I took notice that the fust thing he done was to heave a big blanket kind o' careless like into the chair, an' cover the things clean up; an' then in a little while he says, a-sweepin' the whole bundle up in his arms, 'I'll just clear up this little mess, an' give ye a comfortable chair to sit in;' an' he carried it all - blanket, book, bracelets, shawl, an' all - into the next room, an' throwed 'em on the floor in a pile in one corner. There wa'n't but them two rooms to the cabin, so that wa'n't any place for her to be hid, if so be 's there was any woman 'round; an' he said he was livin' alone, an' had been ever since he come. An' it was nigh a year then since he come, so I never know'd what to make on 't, an' I don't suppose there's anybody doos know any more 'n I do; but if them wa'n't women's gear he had out there that night I hain't never seen any women's gear, that's all! Whose'omeever they was, I hain't no idea, nor how they got there; but they was women's gear. Dandy's Steve is he couldn't ha' had any use for sech a shawl's that, let alone sayin' what he'd wanted o' bracelets on his arms!"

"That's so," was the universal ejaculation of Ben's audience when he reached this point in his narrative, and there seemed to be little more to be said on either side. This was all there was of the story. It must stand in each man's mind for what it was worth, according to his individual bias of interpretation. But it had become an old story long before the time at which our later narrative of Dandy Steve's history began; so old, in fact, that it had not been mentioned for years, until the events now about to be chronicled revived it in the minds of Steve's associates and fellow-guides.

Before the end of Steve's first year in his wilderness retreat he had become as conversant with every nook and corner of its labyrinthian recesses as the oldest guides in the region. Not a portage, not a short cut unfamiliar to him; not a narrow winding brook wide enough for a canoe to float in that he did not know. He had spent all his days and many of his nights in these solitary wanderings. Visitors to the region grew wonted to the sight of the comely figure in the slight birch canoe, shooting suddenly athwart their track, or found lying idly in some dark and shaded stream-bed. On the approach of strangers he would instantly away, lifting his hat courteously if there were ladies in the boats he passed, otherwise taking no more note of the presence of human beings than of that of the deer, or the wild fowl on the water. He was not a handsome man, but there was a something in his face at which all looked twice, - men as well as women. It was an unfathomable look, - partly of pain, partly of antagonism. His eyes habitually sought the sky, yet they did not seem to perceive what they gazed upon; it was as if they would pierce beyond it.

"What a strange face!" was a common ejaculation on the part of those thus catching glimpses of his upturned countenance. More than once efforts were made by hunters who encountered him to form his acquaintance; but they were always courteously repelled. Finally he came to be spoken of as the "hermit;" and it was with astonishment, almost incredulity, that, in the spring of his third year in the Adirondacks, he was found at "Paul Smith's" offering his services as guide to a party of gentlemen who, their guide having fallen suddenly ill, were in sore straits for some one to take them down again through the lakes.

Whether it was that he had grown suddenly weary of his isolation and solitude, or whether need had driven him to this means of earning money, no one knew, and he did not say. But once having entered on the life of a guide, he threw himself into it as heartily as if it had been his life-long avocation, and speedily became one of the best guides in the region. It was observed, however, that whenever he could do so he avoided taking parties in which there were ladies. Sometimes for a whole season it would happen that he had not once been seen in charge of such a party. Sometimes, when it was difficult, in fact impossible, for him to assign any reason for refusing to go with parties containing members of the obnoxious sex, he would at the last moment privately entreat some other guide to take his place, and, voluntarily relinquishing all the profits of the engagement, disappear and be lost for several days. During these absences it was often said, "Steve's gone to see his wife," or, "Off with that Indian wife o' his up North;" and these vague, idle, gossiping conjectures slowly crystallized into a positive rumor which no one could either trace or gainsay.

And so the years went on, - one, two, three, four, - and Dandy Steve had become one of the most popular and best-known guides in the Adirondack country. His seeming effeminacy of attire had been long proved to mark no effeminacy of nature, no lack of strength. There was not a better shot, a stronger rower, on the list of summer guides; nor a better cook and provider. Every party which went out under his care returned with warm praise for Steve, with a friendly feeling also, which would in many instances have warmed into familiar acquaintance if Steve would have permitted it. But with all his cheerfulness and obliging good-will he never lost a certain quantity of reserve. Even the men whose servant he was for the time being were insensibly constrained to respect this, and to keep the distance he, not they, determined. There remained always something they could not, as the phrase was, "make out" about him. His aversion to women was well known; so much so that it had come to be a tacitly understood thing that parties of which women were members need not waste their time trying to induce Dandy Steve to take them in charge.

But fate had not lost sight of Steve yet. He had had his period of solitary independence, of apparent absolute control of his own destinies. His seven years were up. If he had supposed that he was serving them, like Jacob of old, for that best-beloved mistress, Freedom, he was mistaken. The seven years were up. How little he dreamed what the eighth would bring him!

It was midsummer, and one of Steve's best patrons, Richard Cravath, of Philadelphia, had not yet appeared. For three summers Mr. Cravath and two or three of his friends had spent a month in the Adirondacks hunting, fishing, camping under Steve's guidance. They were all rich men, and generous, and, what was to Steve of far more worth than the liberal pay, considerate of his feelings, tolerant of his reticence; not a man of them but respected their queer, silent guide's individuality as much as if he had been a man of their own sphere of life. Steve had learned, by some unpleasant experience, that this delicate consideration did not always obtain between employers and employed. It takes an organization finer than the ordinary to perceive, and live up to the perception, that the fact that you have hired a man for a certain sum of money per month to cook your food or drive your horses gives you no right to ask him in regard to his private, personal affairs prying questions which you would not dare to put to common acquaintances in society.

As week after week went by and no news came from Mr. Cravath, Steve found himself really saddened at the thought of not seeing him. He had not realized how large a part of his summer's pleasure, as well as profit, came from the month's sport with this Philadelphia party. Wistfully he scrutinized the lists of arrivals at the different houses day after day, for the familiar names; but they were not to be found. At last, after he had given over looking for them, he was electrified, one evening in September, by having his name called from the piazza of one of the hotels, - "Steve, is that you? You're just the man I want; I was afraid we were too late to get you!"

It was Mr. Cravath, and with him the two friends whom Steve had liked best of all who had been in Mr. Cravath's parties. It was the joy of the sudden surprise which prevented Steve's giving his customary close attention to Mr. Cravath's somewhat vague description of the party he had brought this time.

"You must arrange for eight, Steve," he said. "There may not be quite so many. One or two of the fellows I hoped for have not arrived, and it is too late to wait long for any one. If they are not here by day after to-morrow we will start. - And oh, Steve," he continued, with an affected careless ease, but all the while eying Steve's face anxiously, "I forgot to mention that I have brought my wife along this time. She positively refused to let me off. She said she was tired of hearing so much about the Adirondacks! She was coming this time to see for herself. You needn't have the least fear about having her along! She's as good a traveller as I am, every bit; I've had her in training at it for thirty years, and I tell her, old as we are, we are better campers than most of the young people."

"That's so, Mr. Cravath," replied Steve, his countenance clouded and his voice less joyous, "I'll answer for it with you; but do you think, sir, any lady could go where we went last year?"

In his heart Steve was saying to himself: "The idea of bringing an old woman out here! I wouldn't do it for anybody in the world but Mr. Cravath."

"My wife can go anywhere and do anything that I can, Steve," said Mr. Cravath. "You need not begin to look blue, Steve; and if you back out, or serve us any of your woman-hating tricks, such as I've heard of, I'll never speak to you again, - never."

"I wouldn't serve you any trick, Mr. Cravath, you know that," replied Steve, proudly; "and I haven't the least idea of backing out. But I am afraid Mrs. Cravath will be disappointed," he added, as he went down the steps, and luckily did not turn his head to see Mr. Cravath's face covered with the laughter he had been restraining during the last few moments.

"Caught him, by Jove!" he said, turning to his companion, a tall dark-faced man, - "caught him, by Jove, Randall! He never once thought to ask of what sex the other members of the party might be. He took it for granted my wife was to be the only woman."

"Do you think that was quite fair, Cravath?" replied

Mr. Randall. "He would never have taken us in the world if he had known there were three women in the party."

"Pshaw!" laughed Mr. Cravath. "Good enough for him for having such a crotchet in his head. We'll take it out of him this trip."

"Or set it stronger than ever," said Mr. Randall. "My mind misgives me. We shall wish we had not done it. He may turn sulky and unmanageable on our hands when he finds himself trapped."

"I'll risk it," said Mr. Cravath, confidently. "If I can't bring him around, Helen Wingate will. I never saw the man, woman, child, or dumb beast yet that could resist her."

Mr. Randall sighed. "Poor child!" he said. "Isn't her gayety something wonderful? One would not think to look at her that she had ever had an hour's sorrow; but my wife tells me that she cannot speak of that husband of hers yet without the most passionate weeping!"

"I know it! It's a shame," replied Mr. Cravath, "to see a glorious woman like that throwing her life away on a memory. I did have a hope at one time that she would marry again; but I've given it up. If she would have married any one, it would have been George Walton last winter. No one has ever come so near her as he did; but she sent him off at last, like all the rest."

The "two fellows" on whom Mr. Cravath was counting to make up his party of eight did not appear; and on the second morning after the above conversations Steve received orders to have his boats in readiness at ten o'clock to start with the Cravath party, only six in number.

Old Ben was on the wharf as Steve was making his final arrangements.

"Wall, Steve," he said, shifting his quid of tobacco in a leisurely manner from one side of his mouth to the other, "you've got a soft thing again. You're a damned lucky fellow, Steve; dunno whether you know it or not."

"No, I don't know it," replied Steve, curtly; "and what's more, I don't believe in luck."

"Don't yer?" said Ben, reflectively. "Wall, I do; an' Lord knows 't ain't because I've seen so much of it. Say, Steve," he added, "how'd ye come to take on such a lot o' women folks, this trip?"

"Lot o' women folks! what d' ye mean?" shouted Steve. "There's no womenkind going except one, - Mr. Cravath's wife; and I wish to thunder he'd left her behind."

"Oh, is that all?" said Ben, half innocently, half mischievously, - he was not quite sure of his ground; "be the rest on 'em goin' to stay here? There's three women in the party. Mr. Randall he's got his wife, and there's a widder along, too; mighty fine-lookin' she is; aren't nothin' old about her, I can tell yer!"

A flash shot from Steve's eyes. A half-smothered ejaculation came from his lips as he turned fiercely towards Ben.

"There they be, now, all a-comin' down the steps," continued Ben, chuckling. "I reckon ye got took in for onst; but it's too late now."

"Yes," thought Steve, angrily, as he looked at the smiling party coming towards the landing, - three men and three women.

"It's too late now. If it had been a half-hour sooner 'twould have been early enough. But it's the last time I'm caught in any such way. What a blamed fool I was not to ask who they were! Never thought of the Cravath set lumbering themselves up with women!" And a very unpromising sternness settled down on Steve's expressive features as he stooped down to readjust some of the smaller packages in the boat.

Meantime the members of the approaching party were not wholly at ease in their minds. Mr. Cravath had confessed his suppression of the truth, and Mr. Randall's evident misgiving as to the success of the experiment had proved contagious. "If he's as queer as you say," murmured Mrs. Cravath, "he can make it awfully disagreeable for us. I am almost afraid to go."

"Nonsense!" cried Helen Wingate, merrily. "I'll take that out of him before night. Who ever heard of a man's really disliking women! It is only some particular woman he's disliked. He won't dislike us! He sha'n't dislike me! I'm going to take him by storm! Let me run ahead and jump in first." And she danced on in advance of the rest.

"Wait, Mrs. Wingate!" cried Mr. Cravath, hurrying after her. "Let me come with you."

But he was too late; she ran on, and as she reached the shore, sprang lightly on the plank, calling out: "Oh, there are all our things in already! Guide, guide, please give me your hand, quick! I want to be the first one in the boat."

Steve rose slowly, - turned. At the first glimpse of his face Helen Wingate uttered a shriek which rang in the air, and fell backwards on the sand insensible.

"Good God! she lost her footing!" exclaimed Mr. Cravath.

"She is killed!" cried the others, as they hurried breathlessly to the spot. But when they reached it, there knelt Dandy Steve on the ground by her side, his face whiter than hers, his eyes streaming with tears, his arms around her, calling, "Helen! Helen!"

At the sound of footsteps and voices he looked up, and, instantly seeking Mr. Cravath's face, gasped: "She is my wife, Mr. Cravath!"

The dumbness of unutterable astonishment fell on the whole party at these words; but in another second, rallying from the shock; they knelt around the seemingly lifeless woman, trying to arouse her. Presently she opened her eyes, and, seeing Mrs. Randall's face bending above her, said faintly: "It's Stephen! I always knew I should find him somewhere." Then she sank away again into unconsciousness.

The party for the lakes must be postponed; that was evident. Neither would it go out under the guidance of Dandy Steve, nor would Mrs. Wingate go with it; those two things were equally evident.

Which facts, revolving slowly in Old Ben's brain, led him to seat himself on the shore and abide the course of events. When, about noon, Mr. Cravath appeared, coming to look after their hastily abandoned effects, Old Ben touched his hat civilly, and said: "Good-day, sir; I thought maybe I'd get this job o' guidin' now. Leastways, I'd stay by yer truck here till somebody come to look it up."

Old Ben was the guide of all others Mr. Cravath would have chosen, next to Dandy Steve.

"By Jove, Ben," he said, "this is luck! Can you go off with us at once? Steve has got other business on hand. That lady is his wife, from whom he has been separated many years."

"So I heerd him say, sir, when he was a-pickin' her up," answered Ben, composedly, as if such things were a daily occurrence in the Adirondacks.

"Can you go with us at once?" continued Mr. Cravath.

"In an hour, sir," said Ben.

And in an hour they were off, a bewildered but on the whole a relieved and happier party than they had been in the morning. Helen Wingate's long sorrow in the mysterious disappearance of her husband had ennobled and purified her character, and greatly endeared her to her friends; but that which had seemed to them to be explainable only by the fact of his death or his unworthiness she knew was explainable by her own folly and pride.

The end of the story is best told in Old Ben's words.

He was never tired of telling it.

"I never heered exactly the hull partikelers," he said, "for they'd gone long before we got back, and the folks she was with wa'n't the kind that talks much; but I could see they set a store by her. They'd always liked Steve, too, up here's a guide. They niver know'd him while he was a-livin' with her, else they'd ha' know'd him here; but he hadn't lived with her but a mighty little while's near's I could make out. Yer see, she was powerful rich, an' he hadn't but little; 'n' for all she was so much in love with him, she couldn't help a-throwin' it up to him, sort o', an' he couldn't stan' it. So he jest lit out; an' he'd never ha' gone back to her, - never under the shining sun. He'd got jest that grit in him. She'd been a-huntin' everywhere, they said, - all over Europe, 'n' Azhay, 'n' Africa, till she'd given up huntin'; an' he was right close tu hum all the time. He was a first-rate feller, 'n' we was all glad when his luck come ter him 't last. I wished I could ha' seen him to 've asked him if he didn't b'leeve in luck now! Me 'n' him was talkin' about luck that very mornin' while she was a-steppin' down the landin' towards him's fast 's ever she could go! My eyes! how that woman did come a runnin', an' a-callin', 'Guide! guide!' I sha'n't never forgit it. I asked some o' the fellers how she looked when they went off, an' they said her eyes was shinin' like stars; but there wasn't any more of her face to be seen, for she was rolled up in a big red shawl, It gits hoppin' cold here in September. I've always thought't was that same red shawl he had in his cabin; but I dunno's 'twas."

"Wall, I bet they had a fust-rate time on that weddin' journey o' theirn," said one of Ben's rougher cronies one day at the end of the narrative; "'t ain't every feller gets the chance o' two honeymoons with the same woman."

Old Ben looked at him attentively. "Youngster," said he, "'t ain't strange, I suppose, young's you be, th't ye should look at it that way; but ye're off, crony. Ye don't seem ter recolleck 'bout all them years they'd lost out of their lives. I tell ye, it's kind o' harrowin' ter me. Old's I am, and hain't never felt no call ter be married nuther, it's kind o' harrowin' ter me yit ter think o' that woman's yell she giv' when she seed Steve's face. If thar warn't jest a hull lifetime o' misery in't, 'sides the joy o' findin' him, I ain't no jedge. I haven't never felt no call ter marry, 's I sed; but if I had I wouldn't ha' been caught cuttin' up no sech didos's that, - a-throwin' away years o' time they might ha' hed together 'z well's not! Ther' ain't any too much o' this life, anyhow; 't kinder looks ter you youngsters's ef 't 'd last forever. I know how 'tis. I hain't forgot nothin', old's I am. But I tell you, when ye're old's I am, 'n' look back on 't, ye'll be s'prised ter see how short 'tis, an' ye'll reelize more what a fool a man is, or a woman too, - an' I do s'pose they're the foolishest o' ther two, - ter waste a minnit out on 't on querrils, or any other kind o' foolin'."

The Prince's Little Sweetheart.

She was very young. No man had ever made love to her before. She belonged to the people, - the common people. Her parents were poor, and could not buy any wedding trousseau for her. But that did not make any difference. A carriage was sent from the Court for her, and she was carried away "just as she was," in her stuff gown, - the gown the Prince first saw her in. He liked her best in that, he said; and, moreover, what odds did it make about clothes? Were there not rooms upon rooms in the palace, full of the most superb clothes for Princes' Sweethearts?

It was into one of these rooms that she was taken first. On all sides of it were high glass cases reaching up to the ceiling, and filled with gowns and mantles and laces and jewels; everything a woman could wear was there, and all of the very finest. What satins, what velvets, what feathers and flowers! Even down to shoes and stockings, - every shade and color of stockings of the daintiest silk. The Little Sweetheart gazed breathless at them all. But she did not have time to wonder, for in a moment more she was met by attendants, some young, some old, all dressed gayly. She did not dream at first that they were servants, till they began, all together, asking her what she would like to put on. Would she have a lace gown, or a satin? Would she like feathers or flowers? And one ran this

Helen Hunt Jackson

way, and one that; and among them all, the Little Sweetheart was so flustered she did not know if she were really alive and on the earth, or had been transported to some fairy land. And before she fairly realized what was being done, they had her clad in the most beautiful gown that was ever seen, - white satin with gold butterflies on it, and a white lace mantle embroidered in gold butterflies. All white and gold she was, from top to toe, all but one foot; and there was something very odd about that. She heard one of the women whispering to the other, behind her back: "It is too bad there isn't any mate to this slipper! Well, she will have to wear this pink one. It is too big; but if we pin it up at the heel she can keep it on. The Prince really must get some more slippers."

And then they put on her left foot a pink satin slipper, which was so much too big it had to be pinned up in plaits at each side, and the pearl buckle on the top hid her foot quite out of sight. But the Little Sweetheart did not care. In fact, she had no time to think, for the Queen came sailing in and spoke to her, and crowds of ladies in dresses so bright and beautiful that they dazzled her eyes; and the Prince was there kissing her, and in a minute they were married, and went floating off in a dance, which was so swift it did not feel so much like dancing as it did like being carried through the air by a gentle wind.

Through room after room, - there seemed no end to the rooms, and each one more beautiful than the last, - from garden to garden, - some full of trees, some with beautiful lakes in them, some full of solid beds of flowers, - they went, sometimes dancing, sometimes walking, sometimes, it seemed to the Little Sweetheart, floating. Every hour there was some new beautiful thing to see, some new beautiful thing to do. And the Prince never left her for more than a few minutes; and when he came back he brought her gifts and kissed her. Gifts upon gifts he kept bringing, till the Little Sweetheart's hands were so full she had to lay the things down on tables or window-sills, wherever she could find place for them, - which was not easy, for all the rooms were so full of beautiful things that it was difficult to move about without knocking something down.

The hours flew by like minutes. The sun came up high in the heavens, but nobody seemed tired; nobody stopped, - dance, dance, whirl, whirl, song and laughter and ceaseless motion. That was all that was to be seen or heard in this wonderful Court to which the Little Sweetheart had been brought.

Noon came, but nothing stopped. Nobody left off dancing, and the musicians played faster than ever.

And so it was all the long afternoon and through the twilight; and as soon as it was really dark, all the rooms and the gardens and the lakes blazed out with millions of lamps, till it was lighter far than day; and the ladies' dresses, as they danced back and forth, shone and sparkled like butterflies' wings.

At last the lamps began, one by one, to go out, and by degrees a soft sort of light, like moonlight, settled down on the whole place; and the fine-dressed servants that had robed the Little Sweetheart in her white satin gown took it off, and put her to bed in a gold bedstead, with golden silk sheets.

"Oh," thought the Little Sweetheart, "I shall never go

Helen Hunt Jackson

to sleep in the world, and I'm sure I don't want to! I shall just keep my eyes open all night, and see what happens next."

All the beautiful clothes she had taken off were laid on a sofa near the bed, - the white satin dress at top, and the big pink satin slipper, with its huge pearl buckle, on the floor in plain sight. "Where is the other?" thought the Little Sweetheart. "I do believe I lost it off. That's the way they come to have so many odd ones. But how queer! I lost off the tight one! But the big one was pinned to my foot," she said, speaking out loud before she thought; "that was what kept it on."

"You are talking in your sleep, my love," said the Prince, who was close by her side, kissing her.

"Indeed, I am not asleep at all! I haven't shut my eyes," said the Little Sweetheart.

And the next thing she knew it was broad daylight, the sun streaming into her room, and the air resounding in all directions with music and laughter, and flying steps of dancers, just as it had been yesterday.

The Little Sweetheart sat up in bed and looked around her. She thought it very strange that she was all alone! the Prince gone, - no one there to attend to her. In a few moments more she noticed that all her clothes were gone, too.

"Oh," she thought, "I suppose one never wears the same clothes twice in this Court, and they will bring me others! I hope there will be two slippers alike, to-day."

Presently she began to grow impatient; but, being a timid little creature, and having never before seen the inside of a Court or been a Prince's sweetheart, she did not venture to stir, or to make any sound, - only sat still in her bed, waiting to see what would happen. At last she could not bear the sounds of the dancing and laughing and playing and singing any longer. So she jumped up, and, rolling one of the golden silk sheets around her, looked out of the window. There they all were, the crowds of gay people, just as they had been the day before when she was among them, whirling, dancing, laughing, singing. The tears came into the Little Sweetheart's eyes as she gazed. What could it mean that she was deserted in this way, - not even her clothes left for her? She was as much a prisoner in her room as if the door had been locked.

As hour after hour passed, a new misery began to oppress her. She was hungry, - seriously, distressingly hungry. She had been too happy to eat the day before! Though she had sipped and tasted many delicious beverages and viands, which the Prince had pressed upon her, she had not taken any substantial food, and now she began to feel faint for the want of it. As noon drew near, - the time at which she was accustomed in her father's house to eat dinner, - the pangs of her hunger grew unbearable.

"I can't bear it another minute," she said to herself. "I must, and I will, have something to eat! I will slip down by some back way to the kitchen. There must be a kitchen, I suppose."

So saying, she opened one of the doors, and timidly peered into the next room. It chanced to be the room with the great glass cases, full of fine gowns and laces,

Helen Hunt Jackson

where she had been dressed by the obsequious attendants on the previous day. No one was in the room. Glancing fearfully in all directions, she rolled the golden silk sheet tightly around her, and flew, rather than ran, across the floor, and took hold of the handle of one of the glass doors. Alas! it was locked. She tried another, - another; all were locked. In despair she turned to fly back to her bedroom, when suddenly she spied on the floor, in a corner close by the case where hung her beautiful white satin dress, a little heap of what looked like brown rags. She darted toward it, snatched it from the floor, and in a second more was safe back in her room; it was her own old stuff gown.

"What luck!" said the Little Sweetheart; "nobody will ever know me in this. I'll put it on, and creep down the back stairs, and beg a mouthful of food from some of the servants, and they'll never know who I am; and then I'll go back to bed, and stay there till the Prince comes to fetch me. Of course, he will come before long; and if he comes and finds me gone, I hope he will be frightened half to death, and think I have been carried off by robbers!"

Poor foolish Little Sweetheart! It did not take her many seconds to slip into the ragged old stuff gown; then she crept out, keeping close to the walls, so that she could hide behind the furniture if any one saw her.

She listened cautiously at each door before she opened it, and turned away from some where she heard sounds of merry talking and laughing. In the third room that she entered she saw a sight that arrested her instantly and made her cry out in astonishment, - a girl who looked so much like her that she might have been her own sister, and, what was stranger, wore a brown stuff gown exactly like her own, was busily at work in this room with a big broom killing spiders! As the Little Sweetheart appeared in the doorway, this girl looked up, and said: "Oh, ho! there you are, are you? I thought you'd be out before long." And then she laughed unpleasantly.

"Who are you?" said the Little Sweetheart, beginning to tremble all over.

"Oh, I'm a Prince's Sweetheart!" said the girl, laughing still more unpleasantly; and, leaning on her broom, she stared at the Little Sweetheart from top to toe.

"But - " began the Little Sweetheart.

"Oh, we're all Princes' Sweethearts!" interrupted several voices, coming all at once from different corners of the big room; and, before the Little Sweetheart could get out another word, she found herself surrounded by half a dozen or more girls and women, all carrying brooms, and all laughing unpleasantly as they looked at her.

"What!" she gasped, as she gazed at their stuff gowns and their brooms. "You were all of you Princes' Sweethearts? Is it only for one day, then?"

"Only for one day," they all replied.

"And always after that do you have to kill spiders?" she cried.

"Yes; that or nothing," they said. "You see it is a great deal of work to keep all the rooms in this Court clean."

"Isn't it very dull work to kill spiders?" said the Little Sweetheart.

"Yes, very," they said, all speaking at once. "But it's better than sitting still, doing nothing."

"Don't the Princes ever speak to you?" sobbed the Little Sweetheart.

"Yes, sometimes," they answered.

Just then the Little Sweetheart's own Prince came hurrying by, all in armor from head to foot, - splendid shining armor, that clinked as he walked.

"Oh, there he is!" cried the Little Sweetheart, springing forward; then suddenly she recollected her stuff gown, and shrunk back into the group. But the Prince had seen her.

"Oh, how d' do!" he said kindly. "I was wondering what had become of you. Good-bye! I'm off for the grand review to-day. Don't tire yourself out over the spiders. Good-bye!" And he was gone.

"I hate him!" cried the Little Sweetheart, her eyes flashing, and her cheeks scarlet.

"Oh no, you don't!" exclaimed all the spider-sweepers. "That's the worst of it. You may think you do; but you don't. You love him all the time after you've once begun."

"I'll go home!" said the Little Sweetheart.

"You can't," said the others. "It is not permitted."

"Is it always just like this in this Court?" she asked.

"Yes; always the same. One day just like another, - all whirl and dance from morning till night, and new people coming and going all the time, and spiders most of all. You can't think how fast brooms wear out in this Court!"

"I'll die!" said the Little Sweetheart.

"Oh no, you won't!" they said. "There are some of us, in some of the rooms here, that are wrinkled and gray-haired. The most of the Sweethearts live to be old."

"Do they?" said the Little Sweetheart, and burst into tears.

"Heavens!" cried I, "what a dream!" as I opened my eyes. There stood the Little Sweetheart in my room, vanishing away, so vivid had been the dream. "A most extraordinary dream!" said I. "I will write it out. Some of the Princes may read it!"